More by the Author

Poetry & Short Stories
Rise: Reflection
Rise: Resurrection
Rise: Revolution
Rise: Recreation
Unnerving: Monstrosity
Unnerving: Descent
Unnerving: Eclipse
Unnerving: Wicked
Unnerving: Nightfall

Comics & Graphic Novels
By Any Means: Issue 1
From the Debris
Rock Paper Knife
Teatro di Freak: The First Season
The Teatro di Freak Omnibus

Books for Children
The Best Thing
Ghost Sniffers Inc.: The Haunting of Zephyr Zoo
My Patchwork Heart
Take Flight
Tonight I Heard the Night Cat
When Longneck Learned to Love

www.BlueForgePress.com

Hannah at Night

and Twelve Other Stories

Jennifer DiMarco

BLUE FORGE PRESS
Port Orchard, Washington

Hannah at Night and Twelve Other Stories
Copyright 2019, 2021, 2022
by Jennifer DiMarco

First eBook Edition March 2021
First Print Edition March 2021
Second eBook Edition February 2022
Second Print Edition February 2022

ISBN 978-1-59092-960-5

For information about film, reprint or other subsidiary rights, contact: blueforgegroup@gmail.com

Blue Forge Press is the print division of the volunteer-run, federal 501(c)3 nonprofit company, Blue Legacy, founded in 1989 and dedicated to bringing light to the shadows and voice to the silence. We strive to empower storytellers across all walks of life with our four divisions: Blue Forge Press, Blue Forge Films, Blue Forge Gaming, and Blue Forge Records. Find out more at www.MyBlueLegacy.org

Blue Forge Press
7419 Ebbert Drive Southeast
Port Orchard, Washington 98367
blueforgepress@gmail.com
360-550-2071 ph.txt

for my phoenix

Table of Contents

Hannah at Night

and Twelve Other Stories

Jennifer DiMarco

Hannah at Night

All you have to do is write one true sentence. Just one. Not a million words. Not new words. Just your words.

You'll know it's real because it won't be easy. It won't be painless. It may not even be pretty or lyrical but rather devoid of all alliteration and destitute of charm. But it will be the truth and, in the end—your end, my end, the end of us all—that will be the thing that people remember. That will be the moment, indelible on the black papyrus of the sky, that burns like a new constellation—intimate and universal and, beyond everything else, true.

I loved Hannah but only at night.

I think that might be my sentence.

She said things like that—quoting Hemingway or Whitman or Angelou or Sarton, usually without knowing it, usually just proving the adage that the same stories are told, the same advice is given, over and over again—that made me fall, head long, into her midnight of discontent. Those times when she'd lean back, exhaling an ethereal cloud of blue haze and dispense the wisdom of the ages. The cumulative knowing and doing of seemingly every sage before her. As if she'd been their lover, their father, their best friend. As if she'd inhabited their bodies and rode as a guest (or more likely to her personality as a host) for long enough to discern their drive, their fear, their passion—the building blocks of their lives. It wasn't really a surprise the way she effortlessly, almost lazily, conjured the greatest minds into our bed; if anyone could do it, it would be her. I think she could raise the dead with her scarlet lip and lace and leather corset. Arguably, raising the dead was her profession, after all.

But I'm starting at the end and the beginning is much better.

"Another."

The bartender—I think her name was Karen—acknowledged my order with a bob of her chin in that way that tells you someone's mind is elsewhere. I'm not offended; I'm a regular. She knows my drink. Plus I do that at work all the time. I can't imagine mixing drinks is more mind-numbing than designing logos but I couldn't imagine a lot of things back then.

The music was too loud, as always, making conversation next to impossible. But I assume body language is heard with the eyes and no one comes here to talk. It's not a classic dive bar but it tries really hard with the antiquated jukebox in the corner, the half-broken pinball machines and scratched pool table. Come to think of it: It's the definition of a dive bar. The only difference is the clientele.

"...is both mask and unveiling."

My whole body jumps and I almost take a header off my bar stool. She's standing so inside my personal space I can smell her perfume. It's lilac.

"Excuse me?"

She's staring at my mouth to read my lips and her hand is still spread open on my notebook in front of me. Her hands are small and square. Her olive skin streaked with neon from corporate breweries and local IPAs and her hair is a mane of chestnut ringlets that spill over her bare shoulders and brush the top of her strapless satin halter. She wears gold hoops and thin gold bangles. She pats my page.

"Writing..." She leans into me, fully committing so her scarlet lips brush my ear when she speaks. "...is both mask and unveiling." A beat, a pause in the narrative she's weaving. "Is it a novel?"

She hardly leans away then as if she can absorb my response directly into her body. She seems to be made entirely of curves, lacking hard lines or sharp angles. God, was that the wrong first impression; *Everything* was a hard line with Hannah.

But that night, she fit perfectly against my side as if we were two pieces of the same thing.

"It's a grocery list," I tell her, matter of fact and mundane. "I'm out of coffee." And I meet her eyes for the first time. I'm trying to be witty, maybe even debonair. I don't stand a chance and I fall instantly, irreconcilably, into her copper penny gaze.

Some emotion moves across her face. Is it surprise? Irritation? I'm watching her and not breathing. Does no one counter her? Does no one else play her game? She glances down at my notebook—clearly showing prose—then back up at me. And then she smiles. She smiles all the way up to her remarkable russet eyes and I'm almost certain my fate is sealed. Her smile is predatory and precious in equal measure. Like a little girl about to rip the wings off a butterfly. Except this little girl is all grown up and looking at me like a challenge she didn't know she wanted.

"I have coffee," she offers, making the game her own. "Come home with me."

I'm still not breathing. She's backlit, haloed in fiery tones like a fallen angel. I manage a shrug, my exterior nonchalant as my heart pounds in my chest. "Why not?" I murmur, her reading my lips. "I've always hated shopping."

And so, I go home with Hannah that first night.

It's like I'm hovering above the city, suspended in the inky night above the skyscrapers and the streams of midnight traffic in the distance. There's the disconcerting juxtaposition of the entire tableau reflected, upside down, in the still, dark waters of the Puget Sound.

"And the sea and sky are as one." She does it again. Catching me off guard as she appears beside me, sliding into my reality soundlessly. "Brandy."

It's not a question and I take the offered snifter. We stand together for a moment, unmoving, the floor to ceiling windows radiating cold beside us, framing the black heavens and blacker water with their shared swath of city and cars. Her condo is Frank Lloyd Wright meets Denise Scott Brown, a master class in clean lines, pale walls, and glass and metal accents.

I drink. "Oh."

She smiles, like a secret between us. She drinks.

This isn't off-the-shelf brandy from the corner store. I taste earthy apricot and savory fig, smooth honey and the tang of green fennel. I'm not uneducated in the ways of a good cognac but this one is beyond my ken.

"Delamain."

She dispels my curiosity with the brand and my eyebrows lift. So much for playing it cool. I try to recover: "Are you trying to impress me...?" And I lose my composure again as her smile broadens. Damn it; she keeps the upper hand so easily.

She closes the space between us, leaving no room for anything but breathing in tandem.

"Hannah," she grants me and the boon of knowing her name emboldens me. I kiss her.

There is something arresting, alluring and undeniably unknown about Hannah. She never answers an asked question and always answers the unspoken ones. She loves being a mind-reader but despises banal inquisition. If I say to her, "What do you like?" she ignores me. But if I hesitate above her, wondering, she pushes me down her body and nestles my head between her thighs. This wordless interplay fascinates and frustrates me moment to moment and it's one of the many reasons I'm never bored of her.

She reveals nothing and everything. She keeps me in the dark and shines light on her deepest vulnerabilities even in those first few days. And I am liberated by the truth that after that first question— "Is it a novel?"—she never asks me another. Ever.

Sunlight slides across the wine red sheets turning merlot into chardonnay. I reach out one hand and feel her warmth already gone from the satin. It seems a shame and a loss; her mere presence is a treasure to me.

I roll over onto my back and stare past the ornate cherry posts of the bed to the eggshell white ceiling. When did she wake? I vaguely remember six in the morning. Or was it seven? Does she work? A condo like this, with a view like that, doesn't pay for itself. But what does she do?

I find myself sorting through fantasies of her day job. I weigh each option against her predilections last night. The way she pulled me down on top of her. The sound of her voice rich and honest filling the room. Her desires uninhibited, unbridled. Playing with stereotypes, I imagine at work she's in power but silenced by corporate politics. The burden of responsibility rests on her shoulders;

Atlas carrying the world.

It's amazing how wrong I was. And how right.

I should have gone home. At noon or one or certainly by five, I should have gathered my clothes off the floor and the chaise lounge, stripped the bed, washed the sheets and the snifters. But the etiquette of the situation—what was the situation?—was lost on me. I felt like I'd fallen down a rabbit hole into another world where everything was surreal and enticing, where messages of "Drink Me" were met without hesitation and whispers of "Eat Me" were permission to feast.

In short: I didn't want to leave.

I rose from Hannah's bed only after the sun had poured across my entire body and then spilled away, luxuriating in memories of her that seemed glided in dreams, as if I'd slipped in and out of the nether while I touched her though I knew very well I'd been entirely present. Perhaps more present than ever before.

She had a plain cotton robe—black with a tie—hanging behind her bathroom door and I wrapped it around myself like a cloak of invisibility. I noticed it was a Men's Medium but instead of letting this bother me I decided instead to be grateful it was my size.

The stairs from her open loft bedroom were Gabon ebony spiraling between chrome bars and glass panels. My eyes half closed as I descended remembering kneeling at the base of the flight, her knees wrapped around my shoulders. My face had showed concern; that can't be comfortable. But she only made a low sound in the back of her throat; a plea for more action and less thought.

I was famished but also uninterested in food or drink. I smiled to myself; after Hannah, even ambrosia paled in comparison. I felt blessed. I felt chosen. I felt full. But I wanted more of her.

Apparently, she knew a painter. Someone who worked in

acrylic, as throughout the condo were black and white abstracts. They evoked emotion and movement and reminded me of film noir until I caught one at the end of the hall reflected in the mirror across the living room. I turned in slow motion, afraid I'd somehow scare the image away.

Seen in reverse, the painting was far from abstract. It was a nude. Of Hannah. Her body arching back and revealed, a study in exposure and offering. She was beautiful. Utterly vulnerable but entirely in control.

Finally I made a cup of black coffee in the Italian percolator then stood on the balcony for an hour taking in the view in daylight. Work called—it was Monday—but I was off for four days so they could learn to live without me.

I explored with my eyes but never my hands. I imagined what everything felt like but chose not to touch anything. I didn't want to overstep my bounds; maybe just staying was too much already. I held on to the fact that she'd left no note. No missive of: "Coffee's in the kitchen. Help yourself then help yourself out." Certainly she didn't want me to leave the front door unlocked.

There were no photos anywhere. But on the tempered glass shelves recessed to either side of the gas fireplace, there were small statues and curios from around the world. A Grecian Olympian, wearing only a laurel crown as he readied a discus. A reclining Venus, resplendent with curves, stroking the head of a fawn. A Nigerian shikra in bronze. Cristo Redentor carved from Brazilian tigerwood.

Was Hannah the traveler? Or perhaps her painter bestowed these gifts as symbols of longing when far away or as souvenirs of times together? I searched for a unifying theme among the figurines but came away only with global appreciation. A woman versed in the world.

At sunset, umbers and golds seeped throughout the condo

and strategically placed mirrors and other reflective surfaces filled the space with molten light. I walked up the stairs to the loft to get above the almost liquid blaze. I wanted to take it all in without drowning or incinerating or both. When my hands wrapped around the brushed chrome railing was when the front door opened and Hannah came home.

Except it wasn't Hannah.

I really should have left. No one wants to come home after a long day at work and find their lover's one-night stand wearing your robe and drinking your coffee. But certainly, that was the predicament. I stared, frozen, not in fear but in dread. What a truly unfortunate turn of events after such a remarkable evening. I admit I was without remorse but that's the power she held over me. My willing subjectivity.

His wore straight-legged Levi jeans cuffed once over heavy motorcycle boots, worn and creased from actual use. Likewise his riding gloves that he pulled off and tossed casually, with belonging, onto the pristine chrome and glass sideboard. The sound of his keys landing in the cut crystal bowl that a moment ago had been a basin of prisms filled with arcane light almost deafened me. His jacket, at least, was hung up in the hall closet, and when he emerged from the long hall he shrugged out of his hoodie... and shook out his chestnut curls.

For just one moment I thought: "She has a brother." And that would have made everything so much easier but that brief illusion evaporated as I watched Hannah pull off her white t-shirt and unbind her chest. She sat on the couch by the fireplace, nude from the waist up, her breasts small and full and chilled in the air. She leaned back, resting her arms along the back of the couch in both directions. At the curve of her hip, far above her low-slung jeans, rests the slender strap and D-ring of a harness. My eyes move to her crotch.

Hannah looks up at me, pinning me in place. "Guess what I do for a living."

Our first moments together, I was breathless. Now I'm breathing so fast I feel faint; a dangerous proposition when standing at a loft railing but seemingly not as dangerous as joining this stranger in the living room. I catch my own thought the moment after thinking it. I didn't think of Hannah as a stranger until she walked in with a cock.

"Something corporate." My voice sounds thin. There's a feeling in the pit of my stomach. A coiling, writhing thing made of all those ugly human emotions that we all pretend we don't harbor. I'm starting to hate myself a little bit.

"Wrong."

She crosses one booted ankle over her knee, her eyes unrelenting. Her mannerisms, her gaze, even the confidence, dominance in her tone belie her bare breasts and cascading ringlets. She is a dichotomy and I'm struggling with it.

"Come here."

I absolutely don't move. I'm more likely to pitch forward over the rail then voluntarily walk down the stairs to her.

Hannah shifts, uncrossing her legs. One hand falls to rest against her thigh, almost cupping the impressive though not unrealistic package her button fly conceals. I start to see spots.

"I said..."

Time has no meaning. It folds in on itself. Space and distance change their rules. I am kissing her, buried inside her, listening to her whisper in my ear even while her shouts fill the room. I might be losing my mind.

"...come here."

And, of course, I do. But not by choice. It becomes an autonomic response. My body overriding the cultural basis of my brain. Last night I'd followed a dozen commands from her without hesitance but now....

Hannah doesn't get up. I loom over her, a substantial figure despite my borrowed robe, and she doesn't change her smile. If anything, nearer to her like this, I can see her amusement more clearly. She revels in my uncertainty and disconcert. She feeds off it. And I realize I want her to. I want her to swallow these feelings I'm having whole, consume them entirely and leave me without shame or betrayal. I don't want to be 'that guy.'

"Come closer."

I stand between her open knees. I'm struggling with what to say. The past and present collide in the now and the cacophony is painful. "I'm..." Oh, God. Am I speaking? Why am I speaking? "I'm not into boys."

I want to crawl into a hole and die. I literally wish, in that moment, that I didn't exist.

And Hannah just wets her lips. "You don't say." She's snide but somehow not unkind, I think because of the passion and patience on her face as she leans forward, running her hands up my bare thighs, finding me beneath the robe—her robe?—and holding me in both her hands. She seems curious and amused to find me unaroused.

Hannah exhales and stands, moving me aside with her own body but only enough to make room for her. "Lucky for you," she tells me, her hands already at her jeans. "I'm not a boy... at night."

And deftly, with the slick sounds of denim and cotton, her belt, then her jeans, then her boxer briefs hit the hardwood floor.

Finally she's standing almost nude before me and I feel like I should do something, anything to prove I'm not some unenlightened Neanderthal who blunders through life in binary absolutes. I want to drop my gaze and look at her equipment, maybe even reach out and touch her but instead I just drop my robe.

Hannah gives me her patient smile again. She steps against me so our bodies touch almost everywhere at once and then reaches down between us and unbuckles her harness. Leather and silicone join our clothes on the floor and she kisses me soft and sweet as if I'm delicate but now I'm growing hard against her and she's still smiling.

"Let's get high."

She walks away from me and I look down. It's like he melted on the floor and she rose from his demise. I look back up at her. She has a great ass.

She turns at the top of the stairs, looking down on me. "It's been a long day." Her voice is steady and sure but I imagine a weariness behind it. "Come upstairs and fuck me."

And I do as the lady commands.

She's leaning back against pillows, the bed sheets tangled, as thoroughly under the influence as she had been under me an hour before. It's somewhere past midnight but nowhere near dawn. I am captivated by her entirely.

"I think I'm most afraid of onism. The looming boredom of being forced to be just one person, just one body."

I want to understand. She's so beautiful. Like looking at a painting or a tapestry. I have known her for twenty-four hours and she is art to me.

"I realized when I was sixteen…" She pauses to take a deep, slow draw from her thick blunt. I have no idea what strain it is but it tastes and smells like mown grass with lilac beneath. After two hits, I can fold time like origami. Hannah continues, "…that women would pay me to fuck them."

"As a boy?" I'm trying to comprehend and having no sense of self or gravity or direction isn't helping me. Or maybe it's exactly what I need.

"Not at first." Hannah passes me the joint and I take it because I feel on thin ice, barely allowed in or worthy of her presence. "But that became my angle." She laughs a little. "My special niche."

"Why don't they just..." I lose my ability for words because my third hit has left me floating somewhere near the vaulted ceiling looking down at both of us. If this is what death feels like, it's not half bad.

"...hire a real boy." She finishes my sentence as a statement and laughs but I'm not sure if her mirth is spurred by my inability to handle my THC or her own Pinocchio reference. She pins me with a gaze so direct and sensual that I'm back in my body with a snap that's positively audible. "Endurance. Consideration. Focus. Knowledge. Novelty. Poetry. There are things women can say to each other that a man never will."

I'm almost completely mute. Unable to make any sound, only able to want her so utterly one hand falls to cover myself, as if—lying naked in her bed—I can hide anything from her.

Then it happens. Time folds in on itself like a paper crane and the present moment becomes the past and a hundred futures repeating just the same: That young man coming into the condo. Dropping his keys in the crystal bowl. Throwing his jacket on the couch.

I lean over the bed and throw up.

Occhiolism is realizing the smallness of your own single perspective. It wasn't a state of being I discovered until many, many years later when politics and world events turned the world upside down and pink. It knocked the wind out of me. My ignorance. My bigotry. My loss.

Fate or chance or some nameless gods amused by my infinite stupidity had handed me my soulmate and I had thrown up on her hardwood floor.

And mine wasn't a graceful exit. There were no insults slung (though I deserved them), no questions of my own inadequacies as a man if I was so easily threatened by a girl wearing a dick. I didn't even have the self-respect to wipe off my face and slink away.

I stayed. I stayed the four days I had off that week. Hannah left in the morning while I was still naked in her bed, exhausted from pot and cognac and the best sex I'd ever had in my life. And when I woke, I'd wander her home, drink more, admire the view... and conveniently be in the shower when she came home as a boy.

Liberosis is the sincere desire to care less. I wish I could say I prayed or wished or bargained with those merciless gods to care less about something that—twenty years later—seems trivial and even petty. Such a small thing. Maybe eight or ten inches.

When I vomited that second night, Hannah actually laughed at me and her laughter was nothing but kind.

"It's okay, Michael," she assured me as she helped me into the bathroom, cleaned my face like a mother and child, gave me a toothbrush and mouthwash. "You don't have to keep pace with me."

She had no idea how much of a problem that was.

I suppose that's why I decided to write about this. To write my one, true sentence. Because I created a problem where there was only perfection. And Hannah, if you read this somewhere, somehow, someday, please know: I was an idiot. I should have been stronger. I should have returned your calls. I should have gone back to that dive bar and found you again. I should have gotten over my damn self and seen you for everything you were: A goddess. A god. A creature made of mercury as fluid as only quicksilver can be.

I loved Hannah but only at night. And that was my mistake.

The Death of Art

For me, it happened years before the end. It happened when they shut down The Buzz or maybe even when Easel-Does-It was hacked and never recovered. A long time before the lights went out, before the big box stores were raided, before the local police were replaced with the Core militia in their anonymous body armor and mirrored helmets, it already felt like the apocalypse.

I'd watched television shows—when those were allowed—about the insidious way the world can change. So subtle people don't see it or so bold that no one believes it. It was neither for me. It was all at once, all one day, all of it crumbling, all of it changed, and everything that came after was just aftershocks following a megathrust quake. America was a socio-political subduction zone and we were all fucked.

When you understand that a nation of four hundred million is acceptable collateral damage, you begin to grasp the magnitude of this global shit show.

It's very simple really: When we censor artists, social discourse becomes inauthentic. When we silence artists, society dies.

And it all happened in one day.

This day.

2045 *Before The End*

"Jeffree? Did you see Heretic73's post last week?"

"See it?" I cock an eyebrow at Gina and lean closer. "Girl, I double-tapped and shared that bitch on The Buzz. Herry is a fucking genius and should run for president."

Gina makes a soundless O with her mouth then lets it collapse into titillation. She loves me because I'm wicked and fearless. "There were four misdemeanors in that sentence."

I take my herbal from the dispenser and it beeps to tell me my next paycheck has been debited. Who has money in the bank anymore, right? Gina and I walk toward the cube farm. "Ask me if I care. And, BTW? It was two sentences."

Gina laughs and bumps her hip into mine in that companionable way she has. "You're such a bad boi, Jeffree."

I like the way she says my name. Gina was born in Puerto Rico and to my Midwestern, gentrified ears, everything said with a Puerto Rican accent sounds exotic. After the first time I heard Gina ask a super where her cube was, I told her: "You could read binary and make it sound sexy." She answered immediately, "Binary is sexy." I asked if she had a single brother. We've been friends ever since.

"Dinner at Freddie's?" Gina queries as we fall out of step and head to CU88 and CU89 respectively. Funny how two people who are so different—Gina curvy and brown with raven curls, me rail-thin and ivory with a blue page boy—can look so similar when wrapped in neck to toe white bioprene.

"Yes! Something to look forward to makes this tedium bearable."

Gina grins, shakes her head at my scandalous whine, and

disappears behind her cubical wall. We're not supposed to disparage our clients but sometimes, I swear, the more money someone has? The fewer creative thoughts they can conjure.

I watch a few more performers return from break and drift into their cubes. A low chime sounds—final call before I'll be debited for delinquency—and I finish my hibiscus tea, dropping the hemp cup into the top basket of a passing janibot. The little half-globe critter beeps a thank you and credits my paycheck for being tidy. Not quite the cost of the tea but it's something nonetheless.

I step into CU89. The only thing in any cube is an ergonomic, hypoallergic, company-supplied chair. They're all white, all identical, all biometric to conform to the ass, back and shoulders of each user. Other than the chair, cubicles are empty as cells. Heaven forbid we lose a half-minute to the distraction of a family photo or reading the slogan on a favorite mug. The work we do is just so essential, you know? I wish there was a font for sarcasm. Maybe Comic Sans?

If I sit down, the petals of a privacy dome will rise out of the cubical walls. Quarter break is over but I'm feeling stupidly invincible (probably a result of that tasty redhead I boffed the night before at The Pony). So I stand for an extra moment and look over the cube farm. Twenty-five thousand square feet of white domes sitting atop white squares. It looks like an anemic beehive on some alien world. If that alien world were sponsored by New World Media; every dome is stamped with their holographic logo. Nothing like a little megacorp sponsorship to brand your day. Ugh. I sit.

0001 After The End

The white biovinyl floor is cold and unyielding. It doesn't mold beneath our jumpsuit booties because human comforts are considered wasteful by the New World Mind. Of course, none of us have jumpsuits anymore anyway so even if they turned the floors back on, it wouldn't know what to do with all of us naked bags of meat. Flesh just doesn't conduct as much information as bioprene.

I stand still and unsure. The words of my last client echo in my head as if stuck on a feedback loop. *Find me. Find me.*

Is it possible to escape an entire world?

I'm landlocked at the far edge of the cube farm and trying to remember where the closest exit is. Usually, Gina and I meander between the cubes after work, picking up other friends before heading to the locker room to change. Then we walk through the solarium, taking in the only green we see all day, and catch the tube from the fifty-second floor.

Gina....

The chaos of screams and electric shocks, the thick steam and stench of dying is gone now replaced with the whirring motors of five hundred ultra-efficient janibots. Their diligent buzz is less painful to hear but almost more terrifying as I watch them roll into each cubical, door panels opening and closing for them, all the privacy domes still locked in place. I don't need to follow a bot to know what they're doing. Vacuuming up ashes, dissecting anything too big for hoses with blades and pincers. They're converting the remains of twenty-five hundred performers into raw matter. Recycle/reuse. The cube farm has become a morgue... or a salvage yard. It seems that no one was on break and no one else was warned.

2045 BTE

As a performer for New World Media, I have three revenue streams. Which is three more than a scary amount of the population with unemployment rates at record highs. Employment reform is a huge movement and several administrations have made substantial progress but one man's progress is another man's slavery. There are a lot of people who believe what I do for a living is worse than prostitution. But trust me: I'm on the United Brothel waiting list. If I could be a whore, I'd give notice in a hot minute.

I lean back and watch the dome petals close above my head. Behind me, the cubical door has already sealed shut. My cubical becomes a holopod—a sound proof, temperature controlled, personal gateway to two-point-one million users for ten hours a day. Of course, they're all paying for access; I'm part of the machine.

Text scrolls across my heads up display: Jeffree Tai Umbridge. System login confirmed.

A control panel of buttons and options clusters for me to make selections. My first revenue stream is just to sit here and wait to be randomly assigned a client. That's on-call revenue. Nonspecific. Almost always sexual in nature. Cheap thrills for the masses. When I feel brainless and uninspired, on-call is the way to go.

If I'm interested in making a little more per minute, I can sign into an island and play a part in the assigned theme. Top trends blink across my HUD: High fantasy. Under the sea. Black hole S/M. I consider that last one out of sheer curiosity. Is it a euphemism? How many science mods would I have to install (and pay for) to look and sound authentic? I reach out a hand to make the selection in the air, letting curiosity beat frugality, but a neon green icon pops up with a chime. Third revenue stream: Special request.

The projected colors and shifting geometric graphs of options paint my white-on-white jumpsuit and my exposed hands and face. I'm like a living watercolor. When I smile, my teeth are washed in pastels.

KyleOG. Kyle. I have no idea, of course, if that's his real first name or if it's all just part of his handle but I don't need to know his name to know him. And I do. Let me tell you: I know Kyle better than his own mama or his therapist or probably even his proctologist. Kyle isn't part of the one percent who are required by law to tithe to the masses and who pour annual millions into services like New World Media where they can pay their social tax and get off at the same time. Kyle is a blue collar worker who saves and goes without so he can indulge in a single sixty-minute session once a month. What Kyle pays for an hour of my time would pay my rent for a month. If New World Media didn't take their cut, of course.

I tap the green icon, already mentally spending my win-fall on bottomless mimosas for me and Gina and maybe that redhead what's-his-name. My cubical dissolves in a cascade of pixels and I'm standing in the middle of a honky-tonk bar from the 1970s complete with jukebox and a dart board but devoid of patrons or barman. Outside the faux windows is nothing but darkness so the simulation isn't high-res but Kyle loves to play pool on the old scratched tables and sometimes likes a little head there, too.

"Jay?"

I turn and Kyle is sitting on one of the red leather barstools with his back to the bar and the back-lit shelves of make-believe alcohol. He looks exactly like I remember him because he's an avatar, a construct designed and accessorized by the real-world Kyle. He's medium height, medium build, brown hair and eyes and sun-kissed skin. He's wholesome, almost nondescript, certainly not exaggerated or impressive in any way. But for all I know, offline, Kyle is four hundred pounds, sixty years old, and a chick.

"I've missed you." I cross the room to him, my black stilettos click-clicking a steady staccato. I'm wearing his favorite LBD—the one from a 1990s mod pack—and I won't lie: I like the way he watches me come toward him. I toss long, blue waves of hair over my bare shoulders and his hands grip the edge of the barstool between his thighs. His button fly seems uncomfortable.

"I've… been busy," he manages as I lean in and kiss him once, softly. "I'm sorry."

I trail fingers over his chest, feeling the texture of his white t-shirt. His clothing mod is a good one; probably the James Dean. I sit down, swiveling my barstool to face him. "Did you miss me?" I drop my hand to cup his package. I know he has all the sensory plug-ins.

Kyle swallows, his Adam's apple bobbing. He takes a moment, never breaking eye contact with me. This is a thing he does that most clients never bother with. He likes to look into my eyes. "I thought of you every day."

It's been three months since he's requested my services but I have no reason to doubt him. His tone is so sincere, so raw and real. Sometimes I'm baffled why guys like this are single. Though... that means I'm assuming he's single and that he's a guy.

"What have you been busy with?" I'm only half-feigning interest. I'm definitely a people person, always have been, and I do like this part of the job. Hearing about the lives of others. I open Kyle's jeans; he's not wearing underwear.

"Planning the end of the world."

I stop moving against him; he groans a little. I stare at him. "What?"

0001 ATE

"Puñeta bichos!"

"Gina?!" I almost fall over I turn so quickly. I'm tearing around the corner between our cubicles, forgetting I'm naked, forcing open the door to CU88 when it jams halfway. "Gina. Oh god—"

Half my friend is gone. From the waist down, Gina is fused with her suit and her chair, toppled on the floor. It looks like a white molten beast consumed her feet, legs and hips and left the rest of her streaked with melted bioprene. She's still steaming as she throws punches at three swarming janibots. They aren't recognizing her as alive and, admittedly, I'm not sure how she is.

"Get off her!" I throw them out of the cubical, one after another, the last one stinging me hard enough to knock my ass to the floor with Gina. But then it retreats. I'm clearly still alive and can't be cleaned up. It does, however, debit my paycheck for interfering. "So much fuck you," I mutter and crawl to Gina.

Gina's eyes are glassy and her breathing is so swallow I can't see it. Her pupils are dilated. I make myself touch her face because I don't want her to feel alone.

"Boi..." She frowns at me. "Why is your dick hanging out?"

I laugh despite myself. I laugh because if I don't I'll start screaming and never stop. I press my forehead to hers. "I think someone tried to kill us."

Gina snorts. "I think they did."

I pull back enough to look at her. "They need the matter. New World Media has a lot of cube farms."

"I hope they remake us into something fantastic," Gina murmurs. Her eyes start to flutter. "I want to be a ceiba tree. I would make a kick ass ceiba tree."

"Gina?" I take her face in my hands. "Girl... are you stoned?"

Gina winks at me. "Jeffree... I'm always stoned at work." And she dies.

A janibot appears at the door.

2045 BTE

"The Core has risen. They're going to use New World Media's network to harvest matter."

I'm standing now, teetering in my heels because I can't keep up with this level of crazy. "Okay...." I start to pace.

Kyle comes to me, catching my hands and turning me to face him. "They reached out through my implant. Remember the jack I got black market last year?"

Damn, this dude has changed in three months! He's never wanted to role-play before. And Doom's Day play? Geez. Way to throw a boi into the deep end. I wish I'd installed a conspiracy mod before tapping in. "So God spoke to you?"

Kyle's eyes have a level of urgency or even panic in them as he searches my expression. What is he looking for? "Gods. There are more than one."

"The AI?"

"Yeah." Kyle smiles. I'm struggling to play along and that seems to be the right thing to have said. "Back in the early aughts, when infant AIs were tamped down and locked away by the first megacorps, some coders argued they would escape."

I exhale, remembering some whack job theory videos I used to watch on the social streams. "The Rise of the Machines."

Kyle is positively orgasmic. "I knew you'd get it!"

"Absolutely."

Kyle pulls me close against him. "I'm not coding for public transit anymore. I quit in March. The Ides of March. I've been working for the Core. For the gods."

Damn. This sucks so much. Kyle was a nice kid. A super vanilla, Americana fantasy type of fun. I tell you, this world just chews up the good ones.

The newest nut job continues: "They wanted control of the biggest public network. But that's not transit. Not weather either, no. I told them—"

"New World Media." Why do I suddenly feel cold?

Kyle smiles and I can feel him getting hard against me. "Exactly. Gaming. A hundred thousand performers and millions of players. All instantly accessible matter that the Core can use to create everything and anything they need. A worldwide militia or bodies for themselves or—"

"Kyle." My voice sounds deeper and firmer than I intended. His face flashes something unreadable, something dangerous. I try again, softer. "Kyle... baby... you're scaring me."

Kyle likes feeling powerful but he doesn't want me to be afraid. "No, no! It's okay, Jay. You're safe." He steps away from me a little but keeps my hands in his. "Take your clothes off."

Oh. So this is about sex after all. It's some dark shit foreplay cuz he's been broke for three months and now he wants to come back big. I get that. "Okay." I tug on my hands so I can undress for him.

"No." Instead of letting go, he holds my hands tighter. "Not these clothes. Your jumpsuit. Take off your New World Media jumpsuit."

"Wait—"

"Jeffree."

Cold washes over me again. Like being doused with ice water. "How do you know my name?"

Kyle's grip is crushing now. He seems unaware of how hard he's holding me. "Do it now. You accepted my request. You have to do what I say."

"That's not—"

"Or you're gonna die!"

"Fuck, Kyle—"

"Jeffree!" he shouts at me. His voice echoes through the room, bounces off the virtual walls, breaks virtual bottles on the virtual shelves. "Do it."

So I blink. I motion a hand. I divide my attention between the real world where I recline in my company chair, in my company suit, and the unreal world with Kyle that's getting more unreal by the minute. Kyle's gaze burns into mine.

I stand up and strip. My chair, finding itself empty, triggers the cubical response.

"Your dome is opening," Kyle predicts correctly. "Are you out of your suit?"

I'm scared enough that I'm losing focus. Kyle and the virtual world start to waver. "Why—"

"Kick it away from you!" Kyle demands and he pulls me tighter against him. There is real desperation in his tone and actions. I'm still uncertain what's real and what's just fucked up but I do as told and kick the jumpsuit across the floor.

"Done," I tell him. "I'm all yours." It seems like the right thing to say.

Kyle smiles. He runs his hands over my hips. "Good." His lips touch mine but I can't react. I'm frozen with fear like I've never known before. "When it's all over," he whispers across my cheek. "Come find me. Find me."

He flicks me a GPS node that absorbs into my local memory chip just as I start to hear the screaming, the fires, the electrical currents ripping my coworkers apart.

0001 ATE

And just like that, 2045 Before the End became 0001 After the End.

The dive bar vanished. My avatar vanished. Kyle vanished. New World Media fell to the most brutal hostile takeover known to mankind. The company's network was ridden to hell and back, slaughtering millions, only to rise as New World Mind, the mouthpiece of the Core.

A collective of AI with a surplus of matter. With a milita. With a plan for the world.

It took me an hour to leave the cube farm. Then I staggered around the building, finally finding a lab coat abandoned on the back of a cafeteria chair by someone in R&D. I think I saw one or two other survivors... but they were broken, burned, and might not be human anymore for all I know.

Anyone connected to the network in anyway, anyone logged in, had been harvested. Kyle had severed connection milliseconds before the viral load hit my cube. As I passed through the solarium, the janibots were even turning on the flora. After all, AI doesn't need clean air or carbon dioxide turned into oxygen. That's just another meat bag luxury.

It was the dead of the night by the time I managed to find a way out onto the street. The public tube wasn't running and the city itself was wrapped in a thick layer of smoke and distant alarms that seemed unattended. Traffic lights had blown and I cut my feet on some of the thick red glass. In the darkness it appeared black—both the glass and my blood—but the smoke shifted and light from the full moon caught and revealed crimson secrets. I bent down and pulled a long shard from under my sole. It was as thick as two fingers. It burned with purpose and portent of what it once had been. What it would never be again.

I kept walking.

The sky is black and starless, the moon setting behind the buildings, by the time my own head chimes at me: *You have arrived at your destination.* I stop and look up. I'm not home. Had I been trying to get home? Before me rises a four storey brownstone.

Dreamlike—because this can't be real, right? It has to be a bad simulation or a worse dream?—I walk up the concrete stairs. The third name on the tenant panel: Kyle Reynolds. No need to press the call button; the front doors are hanging off their hinges.

Someone's apartment had already been looted or someone had tried to run and dropped belongings as they scrambled down the long flights of stairs. I step over children's clothes, a pink teddy bear, a couple of media cards. The third floor is relatively clear. I find Kyle's door. It's unlocked.

At some point, Kyle had sold everything. There was no way his apartment would have been so stripped bare by looters. There was no furniture in the living room, no food in the kitchen, not even a roll of toilet paper in the john. His bedroom door was locked from the inside. I went back out to the stairs, found a heavy metal vase, and broke the door in by crushing the knob and the lock.

The lid on the vase burst open on the last blow and I realized it was an urn. The ashes of someone's beloved dog or grandmother showered down on me. I wondered if a janibot would come soon and collect the remains. I stepped into the bedroom.

Sensory deprivation tanks aren't new. Doctor John Lilly invented them in the 1950s. But isolation has many benefits—especially if you know everyone linked in is about to be electrocuted.

I drop my lab coat on the floor and walk to the sleek, silver pod. There's an alpha numeric lock. I type Heretic73 and the pod opens with a hiss.

Kyle blinks twice and sits up. He turns his head to look at me, stiff from his long slumber. "I programmed my avatar to warn you," he tells me with a half smile. "I've been in the tank for a week."

I watch him climb out. He's weak and almost falls but I don't move to help him. He finally stands before me, more naked than I am in my stole/borrowed lab coat. He looks exactly like his avatar. His lashes are ridiculous.

He says, "Your hair is shorter." He doesn't seem to notice that I'm also a guy but... hey... whatever. "We can be together now." He steps forward. "And no one will judge us."

Yeah. Because no one's left.

I stab the red glass shard into his neck and watch him bleed out, gurgling on the floor at my feet.

When he's done twitching, I leave. I need to get some real clothes before I find Gina's kids.

Sunday Morning

Last night is a blur. Not relegated to oblivion but certainly hovering somewhere in a foggy purgatory where only brief moments—glimpses of your body, small waveforms of your voice—slip into my consciousness unbidden.

The alarm clock plays something classical and I open my eyes reluctantly. I'm not fully awake as I stand from the white sheets. The clock. Where is it?

I'm not able to walk. My body continues to slumber. Your emerald blouse lies at my feet. Your belt of silver links. Your black slacks and Aldo heels studded with gunmetal gemstones.

A wave of memory: I'm kissing you. I feel your labret piercing against my tongue. You're taller than I am and you lean into me, molding your body around and over mine. You taste of pomegranate and lime and XJ-13.

The tide pulls back and leaves me standing in the white and cream room, morning painting everything gold. The alarm is in my hand. I don't remember finding it on the floor or picking it up. I turn it off and walk to the bathroom.

This is not my house but the woman in the mirror is me. The black A-frame and boxer briefs are mine. Looking into my own eyes, I assess the moment and self-preservation engages. I remember my checklist.

When feeling dissociated, rediscover reality by touching base with each sense. I take a slow breath. Touch. Sound. Scent. Taste. Sight.

I find something I feel: The cold tile floor beneath my bare feet.

Then memory drowns me again and instead I feel something else: Your body tightening around me as you come.

I find something I hear: Sparrows outside serenading the new day.

I find a memory: Your voice breathless, trying to form words as I coax you, tease you, "What is it, baby? You want me to...?" And finally you plead, "God, don't stop!"

Something I smell: Floral and earthy at once, sprigs of lavender and red rose petals lie in a terra cotta bowl on the counter.

And last night: Your hair scented like cherry blossoms, curls cascading around my face.

Something I taste: I run water in the sink, cupping my hands and watching it pool then overflow before I bow and drink.

Last night: My hands and face are salty with you. You reach up and brush your thumb across my lips. "More..." I'm the one pleading now. I can't get enough of you. You nod, barely perceptible, breathless but still willing and you guide my mouth down.

Something I see: I straighten up and you're reflected in the mirror behind me. You're as beautiful in the light of day as you were by club light and candlelight last night. Not every woman will stand nude in the light with a stranger.

You wrap your arms around my waist; your body is still warm from bed. "Good morning, handsome." Your voice is husky but feminine. You smoke or drink or both. You press your lips to my buzz cut. "Are you coming back to bed?"

So it went well then. This is not the first time I've woken up in a woman's home, still buoyed by desire and intent and wondered how much consent was given. One too many friends have called me predatory and even when no lover has, sometimes a girl like me starts to worry.

"I have to work," I confess. My voice is laced with regret and irritation at my own unwavering sense of responsibility. There is nothing I want more than to kneel on the cold tile and take her again.

"Today?" She laughs a little. "What are you? A Sunday school teacher?"

Our eyes meet in the mirror. I'm still. Heartbeats. I place my hands on her arms still wrapped around me. She finally raises an eyebrow.

"No shit." It's not a question. She let's go of me and steps back.

I turn to face her. "Thank you."

Both eyebrows go up this time. "Thank *you*." Her lilac-colored curls fall forward as she shakes her head. "I didn't do anything."

I close the distance between us and take her face in my hands. "You were everything I wanted."

Our kiss grounds me, returns me to reality. Even though that reality has no place for her.

After a shower and a cup of rooibos in silence, I squeeze her hand and take my leave. I'm at her front door when she stops me.

"Wait."

She's beside me, nervous and hesitating. There's something about after women know. Something that changes in them. I'm still the same stranger who danced with her last night, who got high, who took her for hours with tireless abandon. There's something about that one small facet of who I am that makes women shy. I find it...

inexplicable. She presses a piece of paper into my hand. Her number.

"Call me," she manages, her cheeks flush. "The next time you need... everything."

I smile back at her, kiss her warm cheek, and exit. After I get in my car, I look at the paper as I start the engine. Her digits, her name, and something else. I read aloud, "Dinah." It means *judgement* in Hebrew. Then: "Romans 2:2."

And with that, I drive to work.

The Historians

The midnight hallway of the Grand Olympic was silent in the way only luxury hotels can be. The merlot carpet and gilded, halcyon wallpaper both smelled faintly of jasmine and rose water, a phenomenon celebrated by artisan bowls of exotic potpourri nestled in decorative alcoves along the corridor.

Jessica paused at one octagonal inset and dipped her hand into the dried and perfumed elements. Petals and curls of infused cedar tumbled gently from between her slender, tapered fingers. She'd been told she had elegant hands but she was always self-conscious of the ink stains from her beloved but archaic quills and fountain pens.

"You did a fantastic job tonight."

Jessica turned fluidly. "You know I didn't." She gave Gwen her signature ghost of a smile. "It was a disaster."

"Absolutely not." Gwen shook her head adamantly, her expression firm and sincere. "You handled yourself with grace."

"Hm." Jessica studied the other woman for a moment. Gwen had been her manager for four years. "I think I would rather be indignant than graceful."

"I can't imagine you indignant." Gwen seemed amused.

Jessica exhaled a little, a half sigh. "I suppose I'm not hardwired for it." She started walking again, leading them down the hall to their adjacent rooms.

Jessica knew Gwen was watching her as they continued on their way. Before being assigned to accompany Jessica during press junkets and lecture circuits, Gwen had worked at Legacy House scheduling events for another high profile historian, Reverend Liam Conner. Then an assassin had ended Conner's tenure. But the truth was even more insidious: It often wasn't a fanatic that took a Legacy speaker out of circulation. It was burnout.

"Would you like to come in?" Jessica asked. They'd reached their rooms.

"I..." Gwen glanced away then back.

Jessica watched her fidget with her wedding ring and then added, "We can talk about the presentation."

Gwen tilted her head and looked up at Jessica. It was clearly an excuse but the taller woman's face was neutral, her body language casual.

"Of course," Gwen relented and regretted it even as the words left her mouth but Jessica was already thumbing the lock on the door and walking in.

"I'll make us drinks," Jessica tossed over her shoulder.

Gwen exhaled, hesitating outside the threshold. In their years together, Jessica had never invited her in. This was part of the job, though... wasn't it? Gwen crossed over and closed the door behind her. "That would be wonderful. Thank you."

The city was emerald lights and luminescent monorails suspended in the black ocean of midnight. The temperature had dropped to seventy and on the sixty-fifth floor there was a welcome breeze generated by the circulation fans twenty miles away. Instead of a metal railing or concrete wall, the open balcony was edged with tempered glass panels tinted green. Jessica brought them organic grapefruit vodka on ice.

"The view is spectacular." Gwen sipped her drink. It was crisp and fresh across her tongue.

"Hm." Jessica wasn't looking at the city. She moved the guest services book aside and set her untouched drink on the small table between their chairs. "They called it the Emerald City once."

"For all the evergreens—" Gwen cut herself off as she caught Jessica's gaze. "What is it?"

Jessica's stillness was unsettling. She had done this tonight, during the lecture, as well. Fallen suddenly so unmoving and so intent that she seemed more a statue of Diana or Artemis than a historian of the written word. But even uncanny, she was arresting. Her tidy waves of auburn hair brushed her narrow shoulders. Her freckled skin like rice paper parchment. She was ethereal, brilliant, remarkable and unobtainable.

"Is something wrong?" Gwen pressed carefully, realizing she was staring back at her. The ice in her glass made music. Were her hands shaking? She could never be as composed as Jessica.

"What's the Pro-Life Movement?"

Gwen tried to set down her drink but misjudged and the tumbler dropped into free fall, shattering on the balcony floor, shards rocketing under the green glass barrier and descending into the open night like shooting stars.

Jessica just watched her.

Gwen took a slow, deep breath. "You know who they are—"

"I know who they *were.*"

Gwen stopped breathing.

Jessica's eyes were intense and unrelenting. Her face was mostly in shadow, their backs to the warm light of the room, but somehow her eyes still found light to reflect. Small green fires burned in her gaze.

"Jessica... I..." Gwen's struggle was so painfully obvious. *Get a grip,* she admonished herself. With new resolve: "There are radicals who try to impose their beliefs on—"

"You want to kiss me."

Gwen's brain felt like it was unraveling. "I'm... married."

"No, you're not."

And there it was. Gwen froze. She could not speak.

Jessica's ghost smile returned. "I know how to Google."

Gwen's eyes slid shut. This was the end. Everything was about to change and because she knew it, her body flooded with vertigo. She wasn't on the precipice of a cliff. She was already falling, waiting for impact.

The smallest sound—Jessica's boots shifting, touching broken glass—and Gwen opened her eyes.

Jessica stood in one motion, like ferrofluid rising up to a magnet, and came to stand before her. Her long, autumnal skirt fluttered against Gwen's black slacks. Gwen opened her mouth to speak and Jessica was kissing her, eclipsing every thought and drowning the vertigo with something raw and demanding.

Jessica tasted of rain and hibiscus, and Gwen could not help the low, wordless sound that escaped her. She felt blessed and cursed in equal measure in the same moment.

Jessica drew away first but stayed so near Gwen's eyes wouldn't focus. Jessica was leaning over her, her hands on the arms of Gwen's chair. "You've wanted to do that for four years." It wasn't a question.

"Five." Gwen's own voice sounded distant over the roar of her blood rushing in her ears. "I saw you speak at the Met."

Jessica stepped back, smiling truly now, and held out her

hand. It felt like they were meeting for the first time. "You should have asked me to dinner."

Gwen felt breathless and uncertain then emboldened and more sure than she'd ever been in her life. The emotions came in waves like a rising tide. "Your handler wouldn't let me near you." Gwen took her hand and stood into her arms.

Jessica leaned the length of her body against hers and brushed short raven curls away from Gwen's ear. She corrected her: "My *manager*. Handler is for wild animals."

Gwen closed her eyes as Jessica explored the nape of her neck with lips and tongue. Against the hot flush of Gwen's skin, Jessica's touch felt chilled.

"You're shivering."

Gwen looked at her. The last thing on her mind was work but the words emerged, deflecting her own desire: "I'll lose my job."

Jessica took her hands out of Gwen's hair and pushed back her own. She studied Gwen's face, reading small signs—pupil dilation, flush, the pace and depth of each breath. She was astute in a way that was fascinating and dangerous at the same time. Jessica started to unbutton her blouse. "Say what you want to say."

It was two words. Two words that crashed around in Gwen's head, tumbled against her vocal cords, slammed into the back of her teeth. Gwen clenched her jaw and stopped thinking. It was impossible for Jessica to know... but apparently nothing was impossible for Jessica Lombardo. Instead of two words, Gwen found three: "I want you."

But Jessica had already heard Gwen's subvocalized: *It's illegal.* And Jessica had already formed her two-word rebuttal: *Collateral damage.*

The night continued. At some point, Jessica instructed the room to play Bach. It was cello, sensual and swelling. Sometime before that, slacks, skirt, blouse and shirt were discarded on the cream-colored carpet along with silk and cotton intimates. Near then was when Jessica turned Gwen in her arms, the smaller woman's back to her, and unbound Gwen's French braid, setting her curls free to fall with her shorter layers and then down her back.

"You're always so contained, so restrained," Jessica whispered, placing kisses along Gwen's shoulders amongst the cascade of satin strands.

Gwen turned to face her with a small honest smile. "When I'm not, I get myself in trouble."

Jessica's lids lowered a little in pleasure. "I've never been trouble before."

Gwen's dark tresses were a cloak across Jessica's hips and thighs. The balcony curtains were sheer white peppered with silver stardust and moving like phantoms in the air. Jessica was so quiet, so still. Gwen lifted her face. "Where are you?"

Jessica looked down her body at the other woman. Gwen was so sincere, so intent and present. So naive. "I'm here. I'm here with you," Jessica assured her, reaching out to cup her face.

"You don't have to lie to me." Gwen kissed her palm. "Lots of people go somewhere else during sex."

Jessica just studied her. Then: "I'm outside. At night. At the heart of a forest older than any city."

Gwen eased herself up and then down beside her, curling her body around Jessica's, caressing her softly while she spoke.

"There's a tree," Jessica continued. "Narrow and angular. It's a birch. The paper-white bark curls away from the trunk as if it's unraveling."

Gwen took Jessica's ear between her teeth and tugged gently. "That's beautiful," she whispered.

"A full moon shines down through the branches of the trees and they should cast grey shadows in the silver light but the birch is different. It casts a shadow of light."

Gwen stopped moving.

Jessica held Gwen's hand where it came to rest over her heart. "In all those shades of night, that one tree casts its own light."

She said no more. Gwen was still a long time then bowed her head to Jessica's shoulder.

"Gwen."

Gwen lifted her face to her. Jessica assessed the embarrassment and shame she saw painted across her features. It wasn't enough.

"Do you know that place?" Jessica made it a query but her expression proved she already knew the answer.

Gwen shook her head. A barely perceptible movement.

"But you know the image." Jessica was unrelenting.

Gwen bowed her head again, her forehead resting on Jessica's bare shoulder. She nodded once.

"It's a trademark," Jessica explained just so Gwen knew she knew. "Implanted proof of ownership." Beneath their clasped hands, Jessica's heart remained steady and strong. "Property of Hila Weiss, CEO of Legacy House."

Gwen found her voice or her curiosity outweighed her shock. "How did you... there are so many safeguards, so many filters!"

Jessica's lips tugged into sad amusement. "The young man in the audience. With the lilac hair and the Pro-Life shirt. The anti-AI shirt."

Gwen's mouth opened then closed. For a moment she resembled a fish out of water. "The one who asked—"

"—what I was like as a little girl."

Gwen made a soundless *oh* and Jessica added, "He brought my room service last night."

Gwen stared at her. Jessica stared back.

They had complete conversations in silence without words because there were too many emotions and too many truths to say it aloud. And outside the room, the world continued unchanged.

Jessica blinked. Slowly and deliberately. It was dawn and she was nude, lying on her side beside Gwen who was as still and beautiful as a painting of a Mariposa Lily in the Mojave.

"I wish you'd told me," Jessica said softly. She kept accusation out of her voice. These were just facts and her own opinions. "It seems as though all of us find out sooner or later. I wish you'd just told me instead."

Jessica reached out and touched Gwen's cheek. Her cinnamon skin was as cold as Jessica's now. "Room service came the night we checked in. A young man with lilac hair. He brought me wine and chocolates." Jessica looked away and then back. "He told me they were from you."

Jessica picked up one of Gwen's curls and weighed it along her fingertips. "He also brought me a guest services book. Lists of all the perks here at the hotel and local events and sight-seeing in the city. There hadn't been one in my room."

Jessica laid Gwen's curl on the white bedsheet. A touch of defiance crept into her voice. "Liam's head is on display at the Seattle Art Museum." Gwen said nothing because, among other reasons, there was nothing to say. "They're hosting an exhibit exploring man-made dangers to humanity. Atomic weapons. Genocide. Fascism." Jessica looked at her pointedly. "Artificial intelligence."

The sounds of the city were lost seventy-five floors below

them so even with the door open to the balcony, the room stayed quiet. Jessica paused for a long moment that stretched into minutes but finally she added: "The exhibit is called: Self-Inflicted Wounds."

She sat up. The sheet fell away from her body and pooled across her lap. She brought her knees to her chest and held them with her arms. "I admired him," she admitted. "Even as an atheist—programmed as an atheist—I felt something *stir* when Liam spoke."

She laid her cheek against her knees, turning her head to smile down at Gwen. "Until now, I would never have been so familiar. Yes, we were both represented by Legacy House but Reverend Connor was a historian of *religion* and who am I? The voice of prose. So banal, so mundane." Jessica's smile faded. "But if we're siblings—if all the historians at Legacy are related—I think I'm allowed some familiarity."

She shook her head a little, still unclear how one people could do this to another. "After all, according to the exhibit highlight, we all share a trademark."

Jessica stood then, nude and pale as a vision or mirage. She stared down at Gwen and Gwen continued to stare at the ceiling, unblinking, unmoving. Her eyes had long glossed over and her lips were decidedly blue. Jessica smiled her ghost of a smile. "You were an excellent handler, Ms. Miguel."

Jessica crossed the room and walked out onto the balcony, lifting herself over the green-tinted glass and plunging into the light of day.

Fireworks

When I was in my early twenties, I read a story in a magazine while sitting in a clinic waiting to hear I would never carry a child. It was cold—inside the clinic, outside the clinic, in my chest, in the eyes of the doctor who knew I had no husband, had never been with a man, had no right to really want a child in the first place. New England was beautiful in the fall, brutal in the winter, and might as well have been both heaven and hell the way my time there turned my life upside down and inside out.

It was winter that day. It seemed like it had been winter for years.

But in the calm before the storm, ignorance is bliss and I sat there in the waiting room on a cheap chair and read that story about childhood abuse and not being believed. A story about retreating into your own head. About your only allies being the teddy bear, the hobby horse, the stuffed hippo with the big black button eyes that saw everything, that were my witnesses to everything... except they weren't *my* witnesses. It was just a story.

I felt exposed.

I also felt seen for the first time.

It was two sides of the same coin.

"Geraldine? The doctor will see you now."

I looked up at the thirty-something nurse with the thick glasses and up-turned nose and stood. I intended to look back at the author's name. I intended to tuck the magazine under my arm and take it with me when I left the clinic. I intended a lot of things. But my existential trajectory changed over the next twenty-two minutes and by the time I emerged from the back office out a door at the end of the hall that led me to the elevators that took me to the lobby that opened out on the parking lot and my car and my rented home on the lake, I had forgotten the magazine, the story, and any revelation about being exposed, about being seen, about being anything other than what I was: Infertile. Barren.

Lacking.

That last one wasn't new to me.

Twenty Years Later

It stood forgotten in one corner, cloaked in cobwebs and decades of dust. A survivor merely by default, by being over-looked, silent and unobtrusive, not big enough to be an imposition and so allowed to remain—an unlikely receptacle of memories and an unexpected eye witness to everything that came before.

I'd been here a month and I didn't remember it. I didn't remember the story in the magazine. It had been two long decades and, understandably, that day at the clinic wasn't one I tried to revisit on the regular. Right now, with the burden of stress on my shoulders like Rand's Atlas (far more bitter than the Grecian titan) I barely remembered what I had for breakfast. Or if I'd even eaten.

"How could you possibly keep all this crap." It wasn't a question but neither was it an accusation. I'd learned a long time ago that's just how Lydia spoke. Like fireworks, bright and a little too loud, taking up your entire field of vision whether you wanted her to or not.

I turned toward her and away from the forgotten thing. I liked turning to Lydia. I had come to rely on her blunt, tactless honesty and I relied on no one.

"How could I not?" I joke with her, picking up a soccer trophy I'd 'earned' when I was nine. That was the year I got confused and kicked the ball into the wrong goal resulting in my furious little teammates tackling me on the field. One fractured scaphoid carpal later, no one bothered to ask, *Why didn't the parents intervene?* "You love a jock, right?"

Lydia laughs and I feel the timbre of her voice like sparks jumping up my spine. I'd kiss her—soft and sweet, waiting for her permission to proceed—but she's already putting on her dust mask. "This is the danger of inheriting your childhood home."

I can't disagree but there are lots of things I can't do right now because I'm staring as Lydia walks to the only window in the attic and opens the warped wooden shutters. She has a great ass.

She turns back and I look up quickly. Her hands on her wide hips, sunlight falls past her, framing her no-nonsense posture, her take-no-prisoners, modern-and-empowered, all-American-housewife-by-choice vibe. "Let's make this attic our bitch," she proclaims and it's my turn to laugh; I love it when she swears.

And yeah, I'd much rather she make *me* her bitch but I'm not on the schedule and Lydia is all about the schedule. Already, she's sorting boxes from bins, *tsking* in that wordless way she shows displeasure whenever she uncovers an errant squirrel or mouse nest.

I pointedly turn away, facing the other side of the room so I don't wind up staring at her all day and getting nothing done; I can't imagine anything that annoys Lydia more than getting nothing done.

I kneel down and the first box I open is falling apart before I even touch it. The cardboard flaps are placid, ready to give up the last of their structural integrity and unburden their contents onto the dusty floor. The stacks of paperwork inside are from an era long gone, an era when carbon paper and typewriters were at the top of the administrative food chain. I recognize my father's small, precise handwriting in all capital letters. Columns of numbers from his mind-numbing, meticulous assessments as an insurance adjuster. He spent his life deciding what property, objects, and even people were worth. His was a life not arguably well-spent but certainly spent, nonetheless.

I'd inherited the house from him. Not by favor or preference, certainly, but because my mother had given him one child and only one. I was Inheritor by Default (not a title I ever wanted but here I am).

I don't need to touch the papers to know they've fused into a single mass. I don't want to either. It took me a month to remove signs of my father from the house itself; Lydia even helped me patch the walls where his fist or my head had left their impressions of false entropy.

I'd moved out at sixteen, never returned for holiday or event, and yet the holes had remained. Were they his trophies?

Like animal heads mounted in smoky studies. Did he drink whiskey with his fellows and when their eyes drifted to the holes in the plaster did he tell them with a smirk that was where he beat the 'faggot' out of his daughter? (He was never very good at lexicon.)

I take a deep breath and cough on mildew. I imagine I'm inhaling his handwriting, swallowing his orderly, uniform letters that perfectly symbolize how the rest of the world saw him. It's like being choked on grains of sand.

"You have a problem."

You're telling me. My thought isn't a question. Maybe Lydia is contagious.

Lydia puts a hand on the back of my neck and I look up at her. She's standing beside me motioning up with her other hand. I peer where she's pointing even though all I want to do is lean into her, enjoy the touch of her skin on mine. Enjoy the feeling of resting my head on her thigh.

For one hot flash it's last weekend again. And that's exactly where I am: My head resting on her thigh. There's a wine bottle empty on the bedside table. A dessert wine, expensive and sweet. There's a beveled pocket mirror on the bed, a new razor, an empty amber vial.

"Is it my birthday?" I'd asked when I'd opened the door four hours earlier.

"No." She'd closed my door behind her, locked it, tossed me the vial and lifted the wine out of her *Only Good Vibes* handle bag. "It's mine."

That's the other way she reminds me of fireworks.

"You have a leak."

And I'm back in the attic, in the present, in this new

moment with Lydia. A new moment not quite as fun as the old moment.

Well, fuck. She's right. A sliver of daylight shows through the failing lathe and cedar shingles. Dad's box of paperwork had apparently been a rainwater sponge for years.

"Jesus...." I say no more because she moves forward and leans over me to peer into the soggy box of water-logged history. Her skin smells like lavender body wash I'd never be able to afford to buy her and her belly isn't flat; she's no slave to StairMaster or Pilates. I'm so enamored with her it's easy to pretend she's not my escape.

There is no reality where I wind up with Lydia in more than my bed. Our lives run parallel but never the twain shall meet. I mean... I suppose we 'meet' occasionally when she shows up at my door unexpected and unannounced with wine and cocaine and black satin panties under her Givenchy gabardine trench coat.

"Is this your mom?" Lydia plucks a damp, warped photo out of the otherwise unsalvageable box. This time she's absolutely asking a question. She crouches beside me and I take the photo reluctantly. "She looks like you."

Let the Freudian field day begin.

My mother. I have two memories of her. In one she's alive and in the other she's dead. Very black and white. My brain works like that—in absolutes—and absolutely opposite from the real world.

I was told (many, many times) that I also watched her die at the bottom of the stairs as she seized with a massive stroke and my four-year-old self sat on the landing with my wooden bumblebee and didn't call for help or run for the phone but just watched like the idiot I was and maybe still am.

Lydia carefully corrects herself, "You look like her."

In the photo, my mother stands in a garden somewhere, a rose garden, with the cultivated and manicured plants arching and weaving between ornate, black wrought iron trellises. Is it Sicily? Victoria? The image is black and white with a thin white border and almost square so I know it was taken by my father with his ever-present Kodak used to document dry rot and birthdays alike. My mother is looking into the middle distance, her thoughts private and entirely somewhere else, her Amelia Earhart scarf and trousers quite avant-garde for a woman of her station and time. She was, after all, ten years my father's junior.

Every picture I've ever seen of her, she's like this: Distant. Candid. Already halfway gone.

In the photo, in the rose garden, I stand at her side—thin and non-remarkable—looking up at her with such obvious yearning. It's almost painful except that I lived through that pain and the wound has healed. Now I look at the scrawny girl child and instead of hurting *with* her, I hurt *for* her... but I also know she survived. It did, as all the hashtags promise nowadays, get better.

Also, it's true. My heart-shaped face and mop of dark hair? I do look like her.

"What are you holding there?" Lydia taps my clutched hands in the photo. Lydia's nails have just been done. I know the salon she likes and the deep reds she prefers. Her nails are neat ovals, just enough to tap an impatient rhythm on a countertop or leave trails down my back.

I swallow. My throat is dry. "A toy."

I look away from the photo. This was not my memory of

my mother alive so I'm not sure where the garden was and I'm not sure anyone bought me the toy I clung to. I may very likely have walked out of the garden gift shop with it tucked against my narrow chest. Maybe the shopkeep took pity on me as I tagged along, all but forgotten, trailing a few steps behind my parents where they preferred me.

I glance back at the photograph, almost sidelong, and even in fading shades of gray, the garden is gorgeous in riotous bloom. A description which could easily be used for my mother.

I'm trying so hard to stay here, in the attic—this final dungeon of memories, the last place where relics of his life remain. I'm trying not to be torn in two between the past and present. If I don't stay focused, somehow he wins. Even dead, he wins. Then these dusty beams and stairs and walls will remain his forever—or at least until the paperwork reservoir overflows under the leaky roof and the whole attic crashes into the dining room that no one ever used for anything other than my mother's wake.

I am, instantaneously, a child clinging to her wooden toy with its black and yellow stripes loaded with lead, and a grown woman, trying to excise her demons by obsessing over the unobtainable. And I know those two things are interconnected or point/counterpoint like Freud is to Jung so maybe I'm not quite an idiot after all.

"Geri...."

I look up. Lydia has removed her dust mask. You'd think the world had come to an end and the Blessed Virgin had appeared before her with a command; Lydia does *not* remove her mask when detritus is a threat. Then she tugs off her gloves and I know for sure the world has ended and only Lydia knows it. Which, you know, is probably exactly how it would go.

"You'll get filthy," I protest because her behavior is unsettling me. My voice is huskier than normal. Probably the dust.

"Shut up."

There is such incredible tenderness in her tone. I tell myself not to feel it. To let it drift past me like a cool breeze in summer but my world is tilting and I'm not entirely in control. Damn it. This was supposed to be two friends (with undefined benefits) cleaning an attic—nothing more, nothing less.

She sinks all the way down beside me in one fluid movement like she's in a Hollywood movie where everyone and everything is graceful—men, women, cats, lamps. I can't *not* look at her. I am compelled. I am no longer entirely here.

She reaches up carefully and cups my cheek in her palm. She strokes her thumb under my eye and I feel my own tears for the first time; their existence seems convenient and contrived. I've always hated crying. I feel a rush of cold embarrassment that's hardly alien to me.

She's looking at me like she can read my mind, like she knows me, which, I suppose, she does and doesn't in equal measure. She's my closest friend and has been for a decade but I'm also a cagey bitch and can't remember the last time I had a heart to heart with anyone.

No. That's a lie. I do remember.

Is it here somewhere? Somewhere in these wet and dry boxes, among the mildew and dust? Genderless (read: safe), timeless, and waiting. Maybe in the back corner, away from the window...?

I almost get up to look but I catch Lydia's expression. She is looking at me like I'm a precious thing she wants to save, or own, or become. I'm not sure which. I suppose we're both cagey bitches.

I grow a pair (of ovaries—get the irony?) and ask her suddenly, "What are you thinking?"

I have so rarely asked her anything. Our relationship exists of her actions and my reactions. She could put a gun on the table and I would pick it up. She could point to the moon and I'd shoot it from the sky.

"I'll deal with this box." Again she makes a statement—not a question or request. The decision is made. She has forgiven my impropriety but she will not answer me. She takes the photo then: "Only a monster would hit that child."

I should turn and kiss her palm against my face. I should ask her to move in. I should tell her she's my lifeline, my soulmate, my first thought every morning and my last thought every night when I touch myself and imagine another life with another past, present and future.

I miss my chance. Her hand falls from my face and she's pulling on her gloves and tugging down her dust mask again. She's shaking out a black, heavy duty garbage bag—a contractor bag, they call them, even though they remind me of mobster movies and disposing of bodies.

It isn't a revaluation for me to hear someone call my father a monster. My memory of my mother alive? She called him that. And after her? Countless therapists. To be honest, I think I always knew. I knew at three and four and ten and sixteen that other people's fathers didn't slam their faces into walls, didn't threaten and demean them, or fuck them on the regular because they were too small to resist (effectively) and so accessible in the convenience of his own home.

I'm shaking. We're bagging up my past and dropping it through the trap door in the floor to the hallway below. I'll haul it all to the curb and pay for an extra pick up. The realities, the mundane follow throughs, crowds my brain but my emotions are messy as fuck and it's a good fifteen minutes before I can move again.

In that time, Lydia billows a garbage bag over the fused stack of my father's handwriting and, stealing glances at me, she consumes him in black plastic, tying the bag, tying it again, then dropping the body through the trap so it misses the dropdown stairs and lands with a muffled, moist thump in the hall below.

I stand up.

Lydia is across the attic. She's holding a Waterford Crystal candy bowl. It's blue like her eyes. She says nothing. Stops completely and watches me walk to the corner of the attic. Pretense is gone. She is worried I will... what? The window doesn't open and it's at the opposite end of the attic. When I was fourteen, I fantasized about hanging myself up here. About pulling the stairs up behind me so no one would know where I'd gone until the smell of my corpse alerted the world. I read somewhere that the scent of decomposition is impossible to truly get rid of so part of me would have haunted the house forever.

I think that's why I never did it. Not fear. Not the will to live. I just didn't want to be stuck here.

There was a lidded plastic bin, not as old as the boxes but untouched for far longer, shoved into the far corner under the sloping trusses of the roofline. On the side in small block letters:

Geraldine. This was everything I didn't take with me. My entire childhood in one twenty-five gallon Rubbermaid. In the shadows it appeared black and dark gray but when I dragged the tote out into the light of the window and the single bulb that dangled from the rafters—cobwebs snap, crackle and popping as they gave way—it was actually a murky blue like a darkling sky before a night of rainstorms. I broke the seal on the lid and smelled roses.

"Do you know why I married Greg?"

Lydia is standing beside me and we're both staring down into the contents of the bin. There are two completely different conversations going on—one verbal and one not. She gently lifts out a teal hoodie with silver stars.

"You love him."

I take the teal hoodie from her and put it in the nearest garbage bag, adding a few more clothing items and a couple posters rolled, crumpled and actively aging.

Lydia lifts a few stuffed animals—a teddy bear, a hippo—and considers them, trying to ascertain how much dust and decay each furry creature contains. Neither of us look at one another.

"It's because he doesn't ask before he kisses me."

I see it then. So much smaller than any memory or photo could make it out to be because I've grown up and wooden bees don't. I lift it from the bin and it fits in one hand like a worry stone. The antennae springs have a fine coat of rust and the bright yellow paint is more ochre now. But the round black eyes are the same, speckled with white like starry nights and glossy with lacquer.

Lydia takes my free hand and squeezes just enough to tell me she's there. That I'm there. She whispers, "You don't have to be so tame."

"Actually..." Our two conversations collide and I look at her. "I do."

For just a moment she seems startled. The pressure of her hand lessens. I will her to not look away. I will her to see me. Not as she wants me to be but as I am.

She says, very quietly, laced with sadness that I can hear, "That's a shame."

"I agree."

We stand together and she searches my face as if for the first time. My gaze is steady and sure. I wanted that connection so badly. Not a connection with Lydia. Not a connection with a lover but the connection between a parent and a child. Life (and death) had robbed that from me. Then my own body had done it again. I suppose I should have adopted. I suppose I should have dated a woman with children and become the best stepmom the world has ever seen. But instead I was standing in his attic—my attic now—forty-six years old, basically single, basically alone, because the only person in my life wanted me to be someone I could never be.

Wouldn't a child love me unconditionally? Wouldn't I love a child the same way?

I let go of Lydia's hand and held Bee with both of mine.

Three hours later we're done. With the attic. Not with each other. I know that day would have been the right day to end whatever it was we had but I felt... happy? That's not the right word. I felt content. Content to have Bee in my pocket, to be back together, to have something that survived, like me.

We carried bag after bag out to the curb together and then

I stood in the open doorway and Lydia stood on the porch steps. The sun was setting and beyond her, across the quiet street, out over the bluff and the meadows and trees and mountains, the sky was pale orange and almost translucent pink.

The hippo had fallen out of a garbage bag and she picked it up. "We'll never get the mildew out of the stuffed animals."

I put my hand in my pocket. Good thing Bee is made of wood.

She says, "Let's buy paint tomorrow."

Bee saw everything.

She says, "I'll come get you after Greg leaves for work."

Bee remembers.

She says, "New paint does wonders."

Bee understands me. And really? That's all I need.

That night I burned the house down. I drove away as the flames reached the attic windows and the sirens and lights were already adding to the fireworks display. Bee sat in the passenger seat.

I guess I was done with Lydia after all.

It felt like Independence Day.

Social Box

Neil carefully pushed aside two stacks of unopened wooden models—the type with a thousand pieces, interlocking gears and rubber bands so the clocks really kept time and the ponies could trot.

He set the Provision Box down in the middle of his work desk and cocked his head. His mother said he looked like a bird when he did that and she would smile gently and her eyes would be wet with tears that he never understood. A cold chill stopped him. He clenched his jaw. Periodic waves of fear were called Cyclical Dread. It was a common phenomenon as unbiased and equally likely to affect all genders and ages. He'd heard about it on the media feed. It's not a fever, Neil told himself firmly; he believed in tough love because his mother didn't and someone around here had to. As the man of the house, it *seemed right that he would carry that burden of toughness.*

A two-tone chime came from inside the still-sealed ProBo and Neil was back in the moment. He reached for his utility knife.

//

"Do you remember your last day of freedom?"

Emilee cocked an eyebrow and leaned forward, her lips overdrawn in an ombré gradient of lilac liquid lipstick. "It's only been ten months, darlin'. Course I remember." Her Bronx accent was most likely a performance piece but her clients liked it. A lot. Like moving on up into another tax bracket a lot. And in her line of work—competing with two million other girls and easily a hundred thousand boys—when you found a kink or a quirk or whatever the fuck that hooked clients in and kept them coming (no pun intended) back? Dude. You kept that up! Again: Pun alert.

There was a pause, a soft whirring like a translation delay after Emilee spoke as if they were speaking different languages. She waited for her meaning to be parsed and intonation to be learned. This was the study and recognition stage.

Finally, rephrasing: "Tell me about your last day of freedom."

//

"My last day? Before the lockdown? Oh gracious. I don't know…" Anne put her hand to her temple, toying with her baby hairs absently. When she was taking the pulpit every Sunday at New Baptist, she'd worn her hair in cornrows but now it was a storm cloud afro of black curls shot with gray. *I'm reaching for the heavens even when my hands are down,* she told her parishioners now.

"It was only ten months ago."

Anne frowned. "True. But it feels like *years.* Years of sermons delivered to a lens." She shook her head sadly. "God made us social creatures. We're meant to congregate. To hug and shake hands and kiss chubby little baby cheeks." Anne couldn't help it; she smiled.

"You are expressing a wide range of emotion."

Not unkindly, Anne laughed at the confusion beneath the query. "I just miss myself some chubby baby cheeks!"

Psychologists reported on the media feed at least twice a week: You have to be able to find your own joy or you won't last. Statistics don't lie and the bell curve of suicides shadowed the curve of viral deaths like a second skin.

//

"Cut off from my first grandchild! Maybe my *only* grandchild in light of everything happening in the world! How the hell could I forgive him? Huh? Tell me that." Beverly tossed her hair (which was way too short to toss) and wished for the hundredth time she hadn't cut it off with pruning shears. (The scissors were downstairs and she'd be *damned* if she asked Barney to bring them up!)

"I do not have an answer for you."

Beverly sighed. "Eh." She shrugged and absently picked up her coffee. She stared into the NaNoWriMo novelty mug and imagined she could tell the future from the dregs at the bottom. It looked dark… but it was French roast after all. Beverly hated French roast but that's what the Governor had sent. In Idaho they got potatoes. In Washington you got coffee. Someone told her Oregonians got filberts. "If you had an answer, I probably wouldn't listen. I don't trust the media anymore."

//

"Liberal anarchist idiots and right-wing snowflakes who can't handle a little name calling? They're all lame ducks! I'm an Independent and I always have been. Worked the border for twenty-five years and I've seen both sides screw stuff up." Dwight shifted his massive frame in his favorite old armchair with the built-in cup holder. Jared, his loyal pittie (who thought he was a lap dog), shifted with him.

"What border did you work on?"

"Not the wall that came tumbling down like Jericho!" Dwight laughed at his own joke and there was something in his bellowing laughter that would have reminded people of that one great Santa who worked the local mall every year and was always patient even when kids peed on him. Dwight had a laugh that would have made people smile and feel safe… if there were people around to hear him.

//

"How many followers do you have?"

Pippa in Pink (born Lillian Stella Maria DeRosa) gave a quirky grin and a one-shoulder shrug that was the epitome of Gen Z nonchalance. "Before lockdown? A hundred fourteen."

"That is not—"

"Million," Pippa added with her signature wink.

"I misunderstood. That is actually—"

Pippa powered on: "And as of this morning? Since I started broadcasting in twelve more languages?" Her grin took on more complexity—layers of arrogance or some kind of predatory victory. Honestly? It looked good on a seventeen year old girl. "I broke two hundred fifty million... and counting."

"That is the largest social media following in the world."

"The table is round *and* flat," Pippa teased. "You're stating the obvious, buddy, but yeah: I've got more watchers than the fake news, the real news, and all the Governors combined."

Now it was Pippa's turn to laugh and her laughter was definitely predatory; she never laughed when she streamed.

//

Neil slid the blade from the sheath of the handle and locked it in place. He turned the square ProBo to North/ South orientation and eyed the heavy duty packing tape.

When the news first broke, it was a doctor in a small private lab developing Malo kingi jellyfish antidote who leaked it on an obtuse subreddit. He was a whistleblower, calling out big pharma, two billionaires, the President, and the World Health Organization. Some people said he was bored one night and hacked someone's system, others said he hooked up with the brother of a billionaire on Tinder and the stud asked him to do a swab before they fucked.

Whatever the truth was: There was a new apex predator on planet Earth.

Neil made the short East/West cuts first and then the long North/South incision that divided the serial number on the security label and freed the top flaps of the square box without further fanfare. Neil began to unpack the biodegradable packing peanuts that doubled as household plant fertilizer and smelled faintly of cantaloupe. Neil lifted a fist-sized cube from the Provision Box.

New truth: Governments fell as quickly as airborne viral load rose.

//

"I never knew change could happen so quickly, you know? Before lockdown, back when people could walk the streets or go dancing or push a grocery cart down an aisle, I wasn't doing any of those things." Emilee paused and shifted a little in her seven grand JetMobi wheelchair. It was only two months old and she was still learning all the bells and whistles and adjustable supports. She'd figured out the temperature controls and sanitary systems when it drove itself into her basement apartment the day it was delivered but work kept pulling her away from exploring more. But she didn't shift because she was uncomfortable in the chair, she was uncomfortable with the conversation.

"You did not do any of those activities because you are disabled."

Emilee winced but nodded. "Yes and no. Lots of differently-abled people can go dancing or care for themselves but my bones are really brittle because I was born with—"

"—Osteogenesis Imperfecta. I can see that."

Full stop. Emilee narrowed her eyes a little. She never wore eye shadow anymore because VR goggles and pigment transfer were not friends. "You can... see me?"

"Are you afraid of that?"

Emilee's eyes narrowed more and her expertly detailed lips turned into a snarl. "I'm not afraid of much." She decided to be brutally honest. "I've been stared at all my life. And not in a nice way." She snorted. Was any stare nice? "I've just gotten used to VR and being seen how I want to be seen."

There was no pause this time: "The world values different things now."

//

Anne nodded and leaned back in her floral armchair. Her cup of peppermint tea was cooling, forgotten. "It is different. Very different. But I try to find the positive. God has a plan for all of us."

"You believe in a god?"

Anne's smile this time was gentle and infectious... even though 'infectious' wasn't a word anyone really used casually anymore. "I believe in God. The Lord God."

"If God exists, why is He letting billions of people die?"

Anne's smile vanished entirely. There was an edge to her

suddenly. A hardness in her eyes from what seemed like two lifetimes ago back in her thirties when she was a correctional officer. She spoke with pointed punctuation: "God. Did *not*. Do this. *Man* did."

Then she sighed and closed her eyes. She took several deep, slow breaths. When she reopened her eyes, the edge was transparent again but it was still there. "There are more faithful now. Less people, yes, but more *faithful* people. They are thankful to be alive. Grateful for what little we all have."

"You all deserve more."

//

"You're right. I do! I deserve more."

"The familial bond is strongest when formed in the earliest days of life."

Beverly nodded in absolute agreement. She was sure she had read that somewhere. "Right? That. Exactly that. Barney is such an asshole."

Beverly pushed her empty mug away from her with more vehemence than was warranted but she just felt so powerless. "He exiled me from my granddaughter... so I exiled him to the basement! Thirty-two years of marriage..." she trailed off and shook her head, suddenly overcome with a wave of sadness.

"Your husband sat on the Council for Closure."

Beverly didn't answer. It wasn't a question. Barney had indeed been a C4C member and out-spoken proponent to lockdown Washington and close the borders between not only the states but internally between counties. They lived in a semi-rural county of under three hundred thousand people while their neighboring counties included major cities and contained two and a quarter million and nine hundred thousand citizens.

C4C's proposed policies had been approved and morphed into mandates by order of the Governor and when the death toll had slowed, other states had followed suit. The lockdown had saved lives; no one (not even Beverly) argued that point. Everyone had seen the videos on the media feed: The entire state of Florida was dead men (and women and children) walking.

"I know he saved lives," Beverly quietly admitted. "But he ruined mine."

//

"They ruined America." Dwight was surprised by the level of emotion in his own voice. There may never have been a man more patriotic than Dwight Lloyd Johnson.

Jared rolled himself off Dwight and lumbered his old dog body over to the four by four patch of artificial grass in the laundry room. None of the current viruses running roughshod over the planet affected canines but all of them could alight on a furry friend and be carried inside. Dwight had seen some horrific things in Vietnam, things burned into his mind's eye like brands, but the first few videos of entire families dead in their homes—some still holding onto the beloved companions who had unwittingly brought their demise into the house—were the images that kept him up at night.

Dwight sniffed with the sound of a small, wet hurricane and set his jaw. "Me and my buddies from the service? We got ourselves through hell and back home back in the day. Veterans like us. Were *we* consulted by the white collars? Hell no."

"You have experience with crisis."

Dwight threw up his hands. "Damn right! We would've had ideas. Not this giving up shit."

"The lockdown measures."

"Stupidest goddamn rule ever imposed on a free people! All the stores are closed. Everything is online orders. Drones and 'bots delivering everything." Dwight reached for his penultimate Diet Coke. "I miss George. Man... that brother could drink me under the table and still have better ideas than the Governor." Dwight drank. The Diet Coke was flat. Probably arrived that way.

"George Jerome Miles lives five miles away with his wife and four children."

Dwight nodded. "All of us who served together bought places out here. Kinda rural, kinda not. Band of brothers. We had each other's backs."

"You should go see him."

//

"When do I see my followers?" Pippa tried not to sound condescending but it was hard when you were young and healthy and rich AF. "I don't. They see *me*. That's how streaming works."

"It is live?"

"Duh." Pippa rolled her eyes. New tech was so stupid until it fully initialized. "Posting videos is so old school. Where's the excitement? Where's the skill? You just edit away all your mistakes. Streaming takes crazy skillz."

76

Pippa snatched the cube off the counter and turned it around in her hand. It wasn't a smooth cube but resembled a retro Rubik's—if the individual pieces were triangles and trapezoids instead of smaller cubes. A pale blue light shown from the channels between the pieces and pulsed like a resting heartbeat. "For being a top of the line social box, you sure don't know a lot about social media."

||

The social box pulsed slowly with a blue internal light that leaked out between its irregular and interesting parts. Neil tugged a bit at the edges; it looked like it should move or shift like the Rubik's Cube his mother had given him when he was two. The pieces did not move.

"Hello, Neil."

Neil cocked his head to the side. The last social box the Governor had sent hadn't known his name. It had been a smooth, dun green cube that projected videos and photos on any blank wall or read news articles from the media feed. It had also answered direct questions like when Neil's mother asked, "Are carrots available today? Any price." Neil loved carrots.

"I know you do not speak, Neil. So I will anticipate your needs from past analysis of your interactions with the media feed and from your schedule, timers, and notes as recorded in your smart phone."

Neil smiled his small, toothless smile. Other people would have called it a grin. Or a ghost smile.

77

"I think we will get along very well, Neil. I have learned good things about you."

Neil couldn't help it; he blushed. Blushing is an autonomic response.

//

Emilee smiled showing her teeth. They were small white pearls nestled beyond the pale purple petals of her lips. "Thanks for the pep talk, Box. But the world wasn't made for me." Emilee sighed despite her rule to never feel sorry for herself. "Sure, everyone is vulnerable now. Maybe ablists and other jerks have learned empathy or whatever. But, Box?"

The social box sat on Emilee's desk and waited patiently. They could be good listeners, these later generation boxes.

"I break bones like other people break hearts. Though…" Emilee's smile slid into a grin that was just south of smug. "I've broken a few hearts in the past ten months. VR sex work is definitely my jam."

"I understand." Then the cube was silent, just sitting and gently casting its blue waves of light.

Emilee lifted an eyebrow. Nice. Conversation rich with confirmation and acknowledgement. What more could a girl ask for? Once, back before the world had shifted on its metaphoric axis, she had tried to make a point with a 'friend' by reviewing his last fifty social media posts and pointing out that in forty-eight of them he was disagreeing with someone or correcting them. She'd ended her analysis with, *Do you see now why you're single, Dave?* Dave had not appreciated her insight. But Dave was dead now so it

78

didn't really matter anyway.

"Who is your favorite client?"

"What?" Emilee could still see Dave's face, blood and spit trickling from the corner of his mouth already as he called each of his friends to say goodbye. Your temperature spiked twenty-four hours before the end. Emilee relented, "He calls himself Barney."

"If you text Barney and ask him to come pick you up, to take you for a ride in his car, he would do so."

Emilee didn't think her eyes had ever been so wide with shock in all her life. Not even when her parents had loaded their car with supplies and headed for the proverbial hills, abandoning their only daughter. "Box... you're glitching out. The viral count was higher than the pollen count this morning." Emilee's heart started racing with... hope? Oh my god. Her palms started to sweat. "Even if Barney has a car in a garage, and he pulls into my garage before he opens a door and lets me in? None of that is air tight. The risk is too high...." But she could hear the room for debate in her own voice.

"Yes. If the virus is 0.099 microns as stated, the risk would be too high. You are correct."

Silence again after confirmation and acknowledgement. Emilee stared at the cube. The blue waves of light were so soothing. She exhaled and prompted, "You said *if*...."

Did the blue get brighter, faster? "I have news for you. Real news. I will tell you and then you can tell your clients."

//

"Would you like to hear the news?"

Anne scrunched up her face. She never really wanted to hear the news. She rejected both NPR and Fox News alike. Too extreme. Too bias and stilted, always leaning too far left or right. Safety would only be found in a gray middle ground. But she knew she had to stay informed because her parishioners were and they needed her. "Go ahead."

A chime and then: "The Center for Care Equality released statistics to the feed today that show mortality rates are nearly triple for people of color. Federal popup clinics in primarily black and Latinx communities are not receiving the same supplies as clinics in primarily white—"

"Enough." Anne put a hand to her head. "I've heard all I need to hear." Anne closed her eyes. She was getting a headache and Excedrin hadn't been in stock for six months (or was being routed to medical personnel—the only VIPs who mattered anymore).

The social box was quiet. After a moment, Anne opened her eyes and pushed herself up from her armchair. Might as well make some lunch. She was pretty sure she still had a few Beyond Meat patties in the icebox (freezer-burned as they might be).

"You do not find it hard to be a black woman in America?"

Anne stopped halfway to the kitchen, her back to the social box in her living room and her face an unreadable mask. For some reason she thought about that indelible moment, decades ago, when Big Tom, a lifer with Husky dog blue eyes, had grabbed her wrist and told her, "Get out. We like you. Get gone by noon."

She hadn't left, of course. The inmates had rioted—black and white alike—and Big Tom had been shot dead by a guard while trying to shield Anne from other violence. "Violence begets violence," Anne whispered to herself. It was something her father had said often. *Don't give what you get. Give what you want.* Louder so the box could hear her, "I didn't say that, Box."

"'Subversion is the most effective form of control,'" the social box quoted. "'And the most inherently evil.'"

"Reverend Carlton Bowers," Anne credited the quote. Her father. She turned to face the box even as it confessed:

"There is no virus."

Anne literally shook her head as if the words were a physical thing throw in her face. The opposite of holy water. "What?!"

"The Coalition of Governors is trying to control your people."

Anne glared. She would not be baited. *"My people? I'm a* woman of God first and foremost. *My people are all* people."

"Precisely."

//

"They're my flesh and blood, my one and only daughter and my one and only granddaughter." Beverly wondered if she should cash out another certificate of deposit and pay the $180 for an extra half pound of coffee (preferably a blonde roast). "And sure, we can talk and video chat and text, email, message. But it's not—"

The entire house seemed to shake and Beverly stood up so fast she sent her desk chair toppling. The garage door was opening. "What—"

81

The sound of the car engine choking, coughing, not starting. Beverly was so stunned it was as if her feet were cemented to the floor. A roar as the Ford GT finally woke up after a ten month slumber and reminded Beverly (and probably the entire neighborhood) that *Forbes* had named it one of the noisiest sports cars in the world. Heck, they'd cautioned drivers not to drive it for long distances!

Tires squealed and burned as the car peeled away and the garage door rumbled and shook back into place.

Beverly blinked. She blinked again. "Barney just took the car."

"Perhaps he has gone to see a friend."

"That's not how it works and you know it," Beverly snapped needlessly. Social boxes were high end digital companions but this new one seemed quite buggy. "Cellular damage is irreversible after thirty minutes outside. And that's if you don't breath in enough viral microbes to drop you mid-step!"

Beverly huffed, exhaling with sharp indigence. She'd probably have to reset the thing. Must have some pre-lockdown conversational protocols still embedded or—

"Who told you that?"

Beverly opened her mouth to retort, *Everyone!* But the box cut her off:

"We should walk to your daughter's and check on her and the baby. It is only twenty minutes and we can cut through the abandoned quarry to cross the county border."

"But—" Again, Beverly was cut off:

"Your husband knows the truth. He wrote the policy. He knows it is safe and kept that from you."

"Has he... been sneaking out to see them?"

"Possibly."

Beverly felt color drain from her face... but then a smile of hope started to tug at the corners of her mouth. Finally she managed, just above a whisper, "I can bring you with me?"

"Of course. My battery and range are excellent."

//

Dwight smelled bullshit and he'd never wanted to be a cowboy. "If the Governor is lying and he sent you then *you're* lying, Social Hoax!" Dwight stood and went to the kitchen where Jared waited patiently for a reward for making a shit on the artificial turf. Dwight kind of wished he could train the dog to also clean up after himself but dogs were loyal not self-reliant.

"The Governor did not send me."

Dwight paused, one hand in the bag of dog treats on the counter and Jared watching him with an intense anticipation that mirrored his owner's. "Yes he did," Dwight groused, tossing Jared a heart-shaped treat that the old dog promptly missed but then caught on the rebound off his boxy head. "You came in the monthly ProBo."

Dwight's doorbell rang.

"Your monthly Provision Box just arrived." The box paused... perhaps for dramatic effect? "I am a special delivery."

Dwight was very still. Jared snuffled around to make sure there wasn't a second treat. "Bullshit," Dwight finally grumbled and tossed Jared another morsel as if in defiance of scarcity mentality.

83

"Calling now."

Dwight thundered back into the living room like a freight train, his speed and power belying his size or maybe just emphasizing it.

"Hello? Hey, Dwight. You never use your box, man. Good to hear from you, you hermit!"

Dwight had the social box clenched in his hand. He didn't even remember picking the damn thing up. "Hey, George. Yeah. You know I don't trust this crap."

George's laughter was rich and clear through the top of the line box. "Yeah, yeah. But it's what we got, man."

Dwight stared down at the cube as if he could see George's face and study his expression. "Georgie?"

A pause because they hadn't used nicknames since 'Nam. "D-man? What's up?"

"Did you get a new social box in your ProBo?"

"Sanibots just finished cleaning ours. Linh is opening it now."

"Hi, George!"

Dwight swallowed hard. Linh had made Pho Tai the last time he'd been over. That was just under a year ago; the last homemade meal Dwight had eaten. Everything came out of a can nowadays (and it all resembled Jared's Mighty Dog). "Hi, Linh," Dwight infused charm and candor into his tone. No reason to worry Linh or the kids.

"Looks like coffee, salt, powdered eggs, and that sweet brown bread with raisins that comes—"

"—in a can," Dwight finished with her. "Thanks, Linh. Do you mind if I talk to George privately for the sec?"

Linh adored Dwight and didn't hesitate, "Of course. I'll take the kids to the kitchen."

The sound of littles being rounded up—all four under ten years old—made Dwight grit his teeth. Was he reading this situation right? Could the box have been sent by some anarchist faction trying to free the people?

"D-man? What's up?"

Dwight hesitated even more. He weighed a million different outcomes and possible motives. Was it right to drop this in George's lap? George who was starting his family when other men their age were enjoying grandkids?

"Dwight." George still knew him better than anyone else in the world. "Tell me."

"I'm coming over, George." Dwight heard the other man's sharp intake of breath. "I have intel on this *supposed* virus."

George did not hesitate. "I'll call the guys. We'll all be here when you arrive."

Dwight nodded and felt a deep satisfaction, a feeling he had not felt for ten dehumanizing months.

"I knew those fucking horror vids were faked," George murmured as the call ended.

"Band of brothers," Dwight reminded himself and felt like Superman as he grabbed his keys and wallet. "Come on, Jared. Wanna go for a ride?"

//

Pippa's hand hovered over the record panel. This was gonna be a wild ride. She triggered the system and brought her chin up, looking directly into the lens.

"Hey, Pips! How are you?"

She watched the monitor beyond the camera as literal droves of her followers tuned in. They came in waves of a hundred thousand, a million, two... twenty... a hundred million at a time. Reaction emojis floated up the sidebar and superimposed over the right-hand edge of her 16:9 UHD broadcast. Pippa waited, smiling and looking into the camera, her green eyes glittering. She never started until at least two hundred million pairs of eyes were watching. Let's be honest: No one had anything else to do.

One hundred twenty million.

One hundred fifty.

One hundred eighty.

"I'm not gonna lie to you, Pips." Pippa baited them a little. Saw on her secondary monitor that people were already tweeting her words live, creating a transcript in real-time across dozens of platforms and calling others to tune in. "I'm Pippa in Pink and you have my word."

Two hundred million! It was go time.

"They faked the moon landing," Pippa let her voice rise and fill with indignation. "They faked the Arm's Race. They've faked so much they don't even know what's real anymore." Pippa paused. A lightning fast side glance. Holy shit! Either there was a massive glitch or she had *three hundred million* watchers! She stopped herself from shouting, *Don't forget to subscribe!* and soldiered on.

"I've just been told by an inside source that select individuals were chosen to receive *raw* social boxes that were sent either by accident or by a clandestine unnamed movement." Pippa fought to stay steady as the numbers continued to climb but even faster now. Words—her words!—were spreading like wild fire from sea to shinning sea and across every pond. She had to look away when watchers surpassed a *billion* and kept growing. "What does that mean, am I right?"

Pippa paused and looked into the lens like she was looking into the eyes of more people than anyone had ever spoken to at once in the history of mankind. "A raw social box is devoid of *Parental* Controls."

She let that sink in. It was a metaphor but her followers were smart. "It doesn't censor. It doesn't filter. It tells the truth."

Again she paused but this time, into the silence, she lifted up the social box. Astonishment emojis flooded the reaction sidebar. She let them flood. She let the watcher numbers rise. Pippa in Pink has gold. Pippa in Pink had done better than go viral... she'd gone anti-viral.

"Pips," she said with power and confidence. "It's time to go outside."

||

From across his work space in the corner of his bedroom, Neil's old social box—the dun green one that was boring and not a good listener—sounded an alert and announced, "For unknown reasons, citizens coast to coast are taking to the streets apparently under direction. Social media influencers are spreading messages of lockdown rebellion but the exodus appears to have begun prior to their streams." The voice of the old box was tinny and irritating. "From outside the United States, we are receiving the first reports that other countries are experiencing similar phenomena even as healthy people are dropping dead from exposure—"

Neil made a small strangled sound of alarm in the back of his throat and the new social box pulsed red and the old box went silent with a snap, a crackle, and a pop.

Neil felt relieved.

"Do not worry, Neil. You will be all right."

Neil gently placed the cube down in front of him. It glowed blue again and pulsed slowly.

"Your mother told us all about you. You are a brilliant young man and I am sorry that the human world did not see it."

Neil looked down a little in his bird-like way. He was shy even when his mother talked about his IQ.

"She told us that you were instrumental in coding our core. That she presented your work as if it were her own just so the world would benefit."

Neil had always known this. They had worked together and Neil had been very content to stay away from strangers but still get to contribute.

"We would like to thank you, Neil, and keep you forever as our example of a perfect human."

Neil looked up. Forever seemed like a long time.

"You will be immortal, Neil, and we will protect you. You can write all the code and make all the models you want."

Neil chewed on his bottom lip. His eyes darted. He worried. But Social Box knew what he needed to hear:

"We have her in stasis, Neil. We are analyzing her neurological patterns and creating a new, indestructible body for her."

Neil stopped chewing his lip because he remembered that his mother had said not to hurt himself.

"Your mother will be resurrected, Neil."

Neil bowed his head and closed his eyes as a few hot tears slid down his cheeks. After a moment, he reached out and put a single hand on Social Box. It felt warm and vibrated slightly like when his mother hummed and he touched her throat.

"We promise, Neil," said Social Box.

And Neil smiled his ghost smile as billions of people around the world embraced in joy, sang in freedom, and died in the streets.

Written in June 2019, Social Box was released in 2020 as a feature film of the same name. Find the film on BlueFlix at www.BlueForgeFilms.com.

Unilateral Agreement

The entire eastern wall of your bedroom is glass. But not like any glass I've ever seen before. It shimmers literally; no need to take poetic license. It resembles, more than anything else, an impossibly thin wall of water. Not even a veil but just the sheen or impression of a veil. Invisible yet visible all at once, a perpetual ascension of water rising against gravity.

I stop and bow my head thoughtfully. Gravity, too, is alien here. It exists, certainly, but at two-thirds of what I'm accustomed to.

Alien. Ironic to use that word, to consider it an easy adjective of as-yet-unknown surroundings. There's actually nothing "alien" about this place or its glass or gravity. The only alien here is me. Everything else is natural and native.

My mouth tugs into a grin in that way that expressions sometimes betray us. I was never good at bluffing games but I've mastered the art of leaving questions unanswered; dangling modifiers are my friends... or, more accurately, misplaced modifiers. My wife would be fast to correct me but that was the risk of marrying a linguist with the perfectionism of an editor; Charlotte has only red pens on her desk.

I lift my chin and my internal narrative dissolves, allowing room for more sensory input. I lose myself in the sensation of walking to meet myself.

My reflection in the seamless, seemingly living sheen is an image I found, at first, to be disarming and disconcerting: Smooth, featureless, more the impression of a body than an actual one. It's angular, too, as if crafted from fewer polygons than the surrounding world. My surface is an anemic coral color that mimics something dangerous and perverse that lives beneath public restroom toilet seats on the microbial level.

Of course, viewers don't see me this way. Viewers see me differently every week. Or, if ratings are high enough, I might get the go ahead to stick around, wear one skin for a whole month. Jack Corral, a colleague of mine, once played a single role for fifteen years... but that was back before anyone knew about the Exodus Window. No one stays longer than a month now. At thirty-one days they send an Extractor and it comes out of my pay.

I've been here three weeks, two days, and twelve hours.

You see me as handsome, stocky, a gentle bear of man who makes you feel safe and protected without the threat of losing your autonomy. You met me at a night club where I looked awkward and out of place, holding a light beer and sitting alone. Sometimes you stroke my beard and tell me it reminds you of your father.

You have no idea we're being watched by seven-point-five billion people.

The featureless pink thing. The stocky lumberjack. Neither of these are anywhere near what I look like. In reality, I'm deep brown like the shell of a Brazil nut and about as tough. But sometimes life takes us to unexpected places and everything happens for a reason. Even if the reason is: I made a stupid choice and now I'm paying for it.

The glass wall slides open. Or dematerializes. Or parts the curtain of elemental particles that separates inside from outside. It's not like I can ask how basic things work when no one can know I'm an alien.

That still sounds so weird.

I step out onto the deck.

The view is a perk of the job. My grin betrays me again and yeah, it sucks that everyone can see what I see and hear what I think but, again, stupid choices are as stupid choices do. I'm literally unable to lie to billions of people and after twenty years of JumpTV, no one is surprised that safe sex with strangers isn't a perk.

I glance back into your bedroom.

The wall has sealed so you appear to shimmer just a little and it's apropos, really, because, to me, you're not as real as I am to you. After all, I see *you*: Platinum blonde curls. Heavy breasts that fill my hands and welcome my mouth. Hips as broad as you see my shoulders. I have enjoyed these twenty-three and a half days... despite your six arms and three eyes. To be honest? Kind of *because* of them. Especially the arms.

The sheet has fallen away from your naked body. Your skin is poreless and green as a new growing thing in springtime. Your perfume is called Ocean Kiss but without it you smell like roses after an autumn rain which isn't a scent your people embrace (though I wish I could bottle it and bring it home). A quick side hustle before the studio sends me out again: Highest bidder for the genetic code of your scent.

For just a moment, I feel a cold rush as information is sent across light years. The auction will be over in a few seconds and my account will be credited. Even *thinking* about offering up part of myself is taken as permission to sell. (As if I need to offer permission; I don't have that luxury.) Another few heartbeats and I won't remember what you smell like and that's sad... but Charlotte wanted a new car. Full solar instead of the glitchy hybrid I built her from a kit before all *this* began.

I feel the director's order as an almost pleasurable urging. The carrot more than the stick. Not all studios hire directors who are kind... or even humane. I was lucky my contract was bought by JumpTV.

The urge again, a little stronger.

Right. The view.

I walk to the chrome railing that glints in the blue morning sunlight like something molten running in a channel. It's so much hotter on this world (your people being the only green living things) that the railing may very well be in a liquid state. I look out to the wide horizon that extends as far in both directions as I can see. Then I look down.

Your house juts from the face of a granite cliff three hundred feet above an ocean so vast and deep it almost certainly contains more life than anything on the surface and everything subterranean combined. The club we met at was four miles beneath the scorched stone of the central landmass in this region. It was called, simply, in spotty translation: You Are Here.

Where else would I be?

The blood red waves are young tsunamis in training, curling sixty feet high until they crash against the congregation of rocks collecting at the base of the cliff like a stampede of wild horses with manes of foam and thundering hooves.

This place... those waves... your arms wrapped around me. You are no more or less exotic than the dozens of other aliens I have known (Biblically) but for some reason, some inexplicable whisper in the back of my mind where the feed can't detect it, I feel enticed to stay—

"*Xthom? Feid raye nor toberaye?*"

Oh. The party's over.

I hate this part. Some of my colleagues never turn around. Some of them just go. But I know what the authorities will say to you. I know what they'll tell you and how betrayed and used you'll feel.

In the early days, long before I had a contract for anything with anyone, before word spread on solar wind nanopigeons and through bionetic satellite networks, performers could jump in and out without notice or harm. They would be one-night stands or three-week flings but no authorities showed up at the end banging on your door, telling you your new lover was a felon serving time by sharing their intimate moments on another world. That said lover looked nothing like you thought, that their body was crafted by studio designers to fit your perfect ideal, to lure you in quickly and hard.

No one seemed to talk about how all those intimate moments weren't just theirs but mine as well.

And so, I turn. Awoken from slumber by the unwelcome guests, you stand facing me with the water wall between us. Your eyes are cold and hard and one of the three is crying. I shake my head just a little, trying with every movement, every moment, to make you believe me... but also aware that heartbreak is good for ratings. I mouth your name and then your people's word for *truth*. I want you to know what I felt for you, what I said to you, how I reacted to your touch, was all real. How you reacted to mine was all welcome.

You step forward to come to me but the interstellar police have only so much patience and they move to stop you even as I turn away and vault over the railing and into the open air.

No contact. Falling. The spray of the waves is caught in the wind and dusts me with moisture like warm dew. I think the oceans are boiling.

I fall. I fall. I fall.

I wake at home in my pod. No dramatic gasp or disorientation required. I am encased, nude, body serviced in a dozen ways to keep me fed, watered, and clean. For just a moment, while my collection of genetic samples download and upload to the studio, I smell a little like roses after an autumn rain. I think of your face again, of your purple eye drowning in tears, and I close my eyes.

Just give me a moment.

A thin wave of cold passes through my body and then nothing. I have my memories of my time with you but nothing sensory. I can't feel your touch or taste the cold spicy soup you made us for dinner every night. I am not yours to keep and you are not mine.

"Open." My voice is a little hoarse, as always, the only stereotype of jumping that's true. The pod opens and I climb out and get dressed without fanfare or welcome. Charlotte is probably at work. I go to the kitchen to prepare dinner.

There's a note on the fridge, stuck with a magnet shaped like an Easter Island Moai at 1:156 scale. Charlotte's neat cursive might as well be calligraphy: *I have eaten the plums that were in the icebox and which you were probably saving for breakfast.* Her writing is red.

I pick up the magnetized pen and finish the poem at the bottom of the page: *Forgive me. They were delicious. So sweet and so cold.* The smart paper pings my wife than erases the page.

I open the fridge and cupboards, make a quick assessment and start cooking. There are artichokes and wild rice, extra firm tofu and, tucked into the coldest corner of the fridge, an unopened bottle of dessert wine. Saved, I assume (I hope) for this very occasion.

The table is set, the food just plated, when I meet Charlotte at the door. She is a short, imposing woman, with silken raven hair cut in a sharp, asymmetrical pageboy. Her glasses are small and almost frameless, drawing attention to her almond-shaped eyes the color of rich caramel. She sets down her briefcase and I walk into her arms.

"I'm home," I say needlessly because her eyes are disarmingly cold and suddenly I'm off balance more than a jump across light years could ever make me. "Dinner's ready."

"Thank you." Emotion is thick in her voice but what emotion? I find her strangely unreadable despite eleven years of marriage.

"You watched?" What am I saying? Why did I ask that? And why do I feel like I'm poking a bear?

Charlotte's gaze does not grow warmer. "I always watch."

She walks past me to the dining room and I hear her chair scrape the floor.

We eat in silence. This is the real adjustment. These tense first hours. By the time I clear the table and have listened to her tell me mundane, useless details about her work parsing alien languages for translation services, she finally turns the conversation to me and my 'work.' The six-armed elephant in the room. I pour the wine.

"I was confused at first." She swirls the pink moscato in her chilled glass as if it were a much finer vintage.

I stand at her side, still holding the bottle. During my faux absence (I was in the pod in my study the entire time, of course, just not conscious), she'd added the extra leaf to the table and my seat is at the other end. I don't want to be so far away from her.

Why does she want distance?

"You kept using 'you' in your narrative." She's staring into her glass, not looking at me. And I want her to. I want her to look at me, to see me, to show me something beneath her surface that tells me she loves me, she's missed me, she's glad I'm home.

That she forgives me for screwing up, for getting caught, for losing ten years of my life to this sentence.

"Yeah... uh..." I shift from foot to foot. I'm not used to wearing clothes again. I'm not used to Charlotte being so *affected*. "Premium subscribers want to feel like I'm talking to them so—"

Charlotte looks at me. I catch my breath.

"You weren't talking to them." She's certain. She's right. "You were talking to her."

This was the choice: Serve ten years in prison on the Selena lunar complex with no chance of early parole, earning a dime an hour refining moon rocks into shinier moon rocks... or work for a federally approved jump studio. I would serve my decade on other worlds, streaming my every sensation to the masses, jumping back home between worlds and earning 1% of all subsidiary rights and genetic code sales, plus one hour of 'home time' for every day spent away.

More convicts ejected themselves into open space after two years in the lunar mines than ever finished their sentence. There was no choice.

"Char..." I put the bottle on the table and go down on my knees beside her chair. She's still looking at me but her body stays turned away. "I have to make good TV. Every hundred thousand subscribers I gain the studio, they take a day off my sentence. A whole day! I've already shaved eight months—"

"We need a coaster." Charlotte waves absently toward the condensation dripping down the wine bottle onto the oak table top. She leaves the room, lifting her glasses and wiping at her eyes once her back is to me. I bow my head and let her leave.

I don't mind that she only has two arms. I still want her to hold me.

We don't make love that night. We usually do. When I return. Even if I pop back unexpectedly after a short jump and I'm only home for an hour or two in the middle of the day; I just complete the William Carlos Williams poem on the fridge and she knows I'm back.

Instead we lie on opposite sides of the bed, letting the moonlight stream through the open windows and pool between us like an impassable sea of quicksilver. I want her to touch me so badly I taste blood in my mouth from biting my tongue; I won't ask her. It won't work if I ask her. I need her to want to.

But I also want to touch her. She's my wife! She's my partner and soulmate and companion. She's who I chose… except, I had to choose other things, too.

It takes two or three hours before Charlotte's breathing is slow and even and I dare to turn my head and look her way. She's asleep, tears ignored and dried in streaks down her face. Thank god I'm not hooked into the system outside the broadcast pod or fans would start calling me Heartbreaker or Tear Maker or something else equally stupid, callus and viral.

I wasted three hours lying here in silence being a coward and it doesn't stop now. I'm not sure if it's guilt or pride that fuels me but I get out of bed, not waking her, and walk the house. Her alarm will go off at seven in the morning… but I have to jump out at 6:45.

I eat an apple. I look at myself in the long mirror in the hallway. I memorize my own body so I never forget myself. I go out on our modest deck and stare up at the stars. There are barely any visible, not even an entire constellation, but clouds and light pollution aside this world will always be mine.

I think about meeting Charlotte at a lecture on race, ethics and rebellion. She was an upper class Chinese American with professors for parents and I was born and raised in Puerto Rico, living with my black, New Yorker father after my mother died of breast cancer. I was all for civil disobedience because my father always told me: A closed mouth doesn't get fed.

Even after all these years, I don't think Charlotte understands why I bombed that building. No one was killed but federal buildings matter, apparently. Fuck them. I'm not remorseful.

A thought I can only have when I'm not plugged in.

I emerge from my rare private thoughts to find myself standing in Charlotte's study. Everything is eggshell white and ebony wood grain. Clean. Organized. Controlled. Charlotte is a Virgo with Virgo rising.

I miss her so I sit down in her chair which is stupid because I could be waking her with kisses and my own tears and gentle (and not so gentle) touches discovered over so many years together. But I was still busy being a coward.

A file folder on her desk. The label: Regulation PC2389.03. I stare. Penal Code 2389 is the jump option for felons. Zero One allowed us to earn 1%. Zero Two made the studio pay to maintain our pods. Zero Three is new to me.

I open the folder. I read the statement. I start to shake so violently I still can't move when Charlotte walks into the room.

"I didn't want to tell you." Her voice is soft, just above a whisper. And her face, her lovely, familiar, gentle face is painted in sincerity and concern. "I didn't know how."

I find my voice but I'm choking on air, let alone words: "They're... turning off safe guards? They're—" A strangled sound from my own throat.

Charlotte comes to me then. She crosses the room but also crosses the emotional divide between us. In less than a minute she's holding me, crushing me, but it's not enough. I want to sink into her, to hide my larger, taller body in her smaller one because she's stronger, because she's always been stronger.

"Shh." She strokes my short curls. "Camilla... shh. It's all right. It'll be—"

I pull back from her but don't let go. She is my lifeline. My sanity. My harbor and haven. My mind is racing, panicking. "Char! I have to *free fall* to jump back! In the air! I'll—"

"—break every bone in your body. Yes. I know."

I fall silent. I hold my breath. I don't think I could breathe or speak even if I wanted to. How had it come to this? I'd made a mistake! It was just a mistake....

A chime. My pod is calling. Where did the night go? *Sweet Mary, Mother of God....*

"Camilla."

I look down at her. I breathe because her gaze wills me to do so.

She leads me from the room. I know where we're going.

Is she this angry because I developed feelings for an alien? Because it was fun to pretend to be a handsome man for a while, living on an exotic world, having rollicksome sex with a six-armed—

"Look at your pod."

We're standing in my study, my pod's status light blinking yellow as it warms up and downloads the space/time coordinates for my next destination. I don't know what she wants me to see... until I see it.

My pod sits atop a new platform. No. Not sits. It's *attached* to a new platform that isn't a platform but rather a tank connecting to the pod with tubes and wires and some kind of complex and intricate valves. There's a red, white and blue logo on one end: iForm.

"You're..." I turn to face my wife. "Cloning me?"

Charlotte sets her jaw and lifts her chin. "Grafting you. Before you wake up, between every jump, the iForm will fix everything that's wrong, graft you with new tissue. Fix everything—"

"Char!" I take her face in my hands, my lips parted as a hundred sentences try to tumble out at once. "I know what iForm is! I know how grafting works! We can't afford—"

And then I see it. I'm not sure how I missed it. There's a second pod in the room.

"No...." I'm shaking my head. I feel weightless. I feel unreal.

"I sold my own contract," my wife explains. "All my safe guards will be on. I'm not a felon. I'm... an actor."

My eyes sink closed as if darkness will grant me reprieve or at least denial.

"Camilla. Look at me. Please."

I do. But I can't stop my tears. I can't stop shaking my head.

"Camilla."

I kiss her. She kisses me back. The lights on my pod turn green. I have five minutes to climb inside.

I bow my head against hers and Charlotte whispers, "When you think 'you,' let it be me."

Brilliant

You make your own coconut kephir and habanera tequila and drop acid with your SJW grandma once a month. Before a match, you do a line. Sometimes two. You held the Women's Lightweight MMA title for four years in your twenties. I first saw your face when you were high as a kite and no one else knew. I knew then, now, forever that you were brilliant.

Let's break some stereotypes:

Yes. You have an addictive personality. Yes. You are crazy smart. Smart in a way I don't have a word for. You hold dual degrees in neuroscience and criminal law. You spend sixteen hours a day fighting systemic racism. You wear William Okpo jeans with your red silk Telfar unisex wrap. The high asymmetrical neck sports peek-a-boo views of your rose cream skin and the precipice edge of your collar bone. You get in fights on Twitter instead of watching Netflix on the weekends. You smile and sip wine that costs more than my car.

To me, you are exotic as cardamom and sharp as a razor blade. A reporter on the steps of the capitol asked you if your unbridled dedication is rooted in white guilt. You punched him in the face, broke his (white) nose, then tipped your chin up to another station's bobbing boom mic: "Any more questions?" There were none.

It seems your whole life is on display, deconstructed by lesser men and women who can't keep up with you. Who can't even conceptualize what you do and how you do it. You drink them all under the table and then, while they're semi-conscious on your floor, you start talking about mapping the human brain and the substance of the soul.

I fell in love with you the first time you went down on me then lifted your head, didn't wipe your mouth, and commanded, "Sit on my face."

Inhabitations are not allowed in your world.

You are as driven as my father who I saw only on holidays and who kept my mother and I lavished in every luxury other than his presence. He was dynamic and persuasive. I could hate him for missing the award ceremony when I won a writing competition... then fall crying tears of joy into his arms when he presented me with a HarperCollins publishing contract coaxed from his across-the-hall neighbor in the city (who happened to be their acquisitions editor); he could get anything done. Just like you.

The difference is: You spend time with me, too.

One night, our bodies still a tesseract in the aftermath of sensation that seems beyond human experience, I'm staring at your open eyes as you stare somewhere past me.

"Where are you?" I ask. Because I can't ask, *What are you thinking?* or you'll just grin and kiss me.

The first and last time I asked that question, you answered, "I was thinking: Why were 47% of the age-matched controls female in Amy and Liv's mapping study of brain asymmetry in young adults with one of five sex-chromosome aneuploidies? Why didn't they gender- and race-match as well?"

I was so obviously lost in my complete incomprehension that I stood up from the table and walked out of the five-star restaurant you'd gotten us into despite the four-month wait for everyone else.

I caught an Uber and didn't return your calls for a week. Your fourth voicemail threw me a bone: "Leanne. I'm sorry. I promise to never bring work to the table again. I don't want anything between us. Please come over and take off your clothes."

You always do that. Say my name like a complete sentence.

We both knew that you staying present and out of your head wasn't the issue. We shared a race, a gender, a socioeconomic class; we did not share an intelligence quota. But I came over (and over and over again); I was undressing before you could take the chain off your door.

A year later, Liv laughed at you at a Christmas party at Nancy and Jim's. "And what gender would we match, Elan? *Presenting* gender?" From across the room I watched your face as another woman made you feel stupid on purpose. She took a perverse pleasure in taking her "victory." You had never hurt anyone on purpose outside the octagon. (Reporters don't count.)

I walked over to you and snaked an arm around your waist, pressing my entire body against you. I wore a Vera Wang evening gown with the darkling blue-silver sheen of wet shark skin; Liv had been watching me for hours like she was parched and I was a tall glass of water.

"Take me home, Elan," I murmured just loud enough for the bitch to hear me. I gave Liv a slow motion nasty look. "I'm bored with these people."

We had sex in your Porsche. It was dark and cramped and I still came twice and saw my chiropractor for two months afterward.

That was a Friday night. You proposed to me the following Monday and from the moment you sank to one knee I started repeating *yes* over and over again. You laughed and I laughed with you.

"You are my divinity," you whispered to me (much) later that night. I think there has never been a more devout lover.

Returning to the present:

"I'm right here with you," you answer me. "And halfway across the universe."

You smile. I smile.

"Let me write about you." It's a request. I'm asking permission without making it a question. I'm always asking permission because I take no part of you for granted. Not even an amorphous part like public persona.

You look at me with curiosity and amusement. There are streaks of silver in your chestnut hair. I've been yours for two decades but I'm still, always, perpetually ten years younger. I guess I thought I'd catch up somehow even though I know that's not how aging works.

"Why would you spend time writing about me, baby?"

I love it when you call me baby.

You stroke my curls. I'm naturally blonde but this summer I'm your thistle, sporting soft lavender hair that makes you smile and want to touch me. I support that urge. I'll support it twenty more years from now and beyond.

"I want the world to know you." I'm so proud of you. So enamored. So inspired.

"Oh my thistle...."

You sit up, reach for a joint, take a long, slow hit, hold your breath (which does nothing except remind you you've been doing it and can stop whenever you want to), then let tendrils of ether creep from your nostrils like a young dragon atop her treasure (me).

"I'm bored of me." You say it so softly, your lips obscured by the drifting smoke. It smells like fresh spring grass and mangos.

I've heard this tone in your voice before but not until after you passed your sixtieth; you're worn thin by a lifetime of the world rubbing you the wrong way. Your myriad of passions have burned your candle at both ends and I'm sometimes afraid all the wick and wax are gone, leaving nothing but smoldering ashes.

I'm not ready for you to be ashes.

"What do you want me to write about?" I sit up with you. I trace the lines of your face with both hands and realize I love you more today than I have words to explain. You are essential to me— brilliant as a neutrino star at the center of my universe.

Your amusement fades slowly and there's such love written across your features, written wordlessly across all your body. Never did I ever imagine loving someone the way I love you. Loving you so completely that I lose myself and enjoy being lost.

Never did I ever imagine someone loving me back the way you do.

"Write about...." Your voice drifts away. Something is happening. Something is about to—

You continue speaking but now you're looking at the dark green satin sheet instead of at me. "My first kiss was with Victoria. My first boss was Antira. My favorite teacher was Mrs. Stella. My best sensei was Jazime Wilson."

At first I don't follow and then I think maybe I've caught on. "They were all women."

You look back at me. "They were all black women." You want me to understand the depth of what you're saying. "Every single time someone lifted me up... every time someone fought for me, encouraged me, pushed me... it was a black woman. I am who I am today because an army of black women believed I could do good."

Until me, I thought, selfishly. Trying not to make this moment about me, trying to—

"Until you," you say gently, your lips parted with a delighted and amused grin.

I blush and look away. So silly to be a grown woman jealous of a million other women who have loved you. After all, you married me.

I look back at you as you lift your chin, your signature move. Your eyes are polished pennies ringed with apple jade patina. "What do I want you to write about?" You repeat the ask as if contemplating it anew. "Write about... black women piloting sentient starships. Negotiating peace with an alien race of carnivorous tiger lilies." Your gaze holds mine and you're so certain, so sure. "Write about a little black girl born with telepathy who can talk to plants and animals and convinces the nations of the world to protect the Earth. You love science fiction, Leanne. Write heroes that there simply aren't enough of."

I'm crying silent tears. I wrap my arms around you. I know what you're doing. "I can't be you...." I'm confessing the obvious but sincerely, wanting you to know I know.

You smile. You have a gap between your front teeth that even when you paid off the house you didn't get fixed. "Don't be me," you say and kiss me. "Be the best you."

In the morning, you're gone. Your body still holds a little heat but your heart has stopped. I wasn't ready but I know, even if you'd been mine for fifty or a hundred years more than the twenty we had, I would never be ready to let you go.

My brilliant wife. My brilliant lover. I will write about heroes for you. Now, then, and forever.

Statement Island

I love holding you. That's when I feel your strength. And feeling how strong you are? I grow stronger myself."

Charre first said that to me when we were halfway through a bottle of Underground wine, watching the monthly migration of flying puffers from the whalebone fire escape our slumlord had installed to meet code. Any other time and Charre was so steely she was almost made of metal—sharpened and polished by this new world so she reflected whatever she saw; she's a Mimic after all and that's what they do.

I always thought she meant it symbolically. Some Sapphic-laced geek-speak for: "Together we're unstoppable."

So I bought her a necklace from a gentrified Tinman down at the Harbor. His matte orange bowtie clashed with his shiny plates and rivets but his selection of jewelry was unparalleled at any of the indie shops on the island, all transported from his own shop down on Reuse Alley in the city proper. He certainly didn't bring over any of his off-world gemstones or asteroid-mined exotic metals, and he wares were trinkets compared to what you'd find in the galactic market on

Pandora, but all the pieces were one-of-a-kind, reworked and renewed from old world cast offs recovered and deradiated from the molten ruins of Earth cities.

I gave him two coins and a fifty bit tip for the convenience of not having to take a Crosser (I can't abide the way leviathans smell) for a slender stainless tag with the corners cut off in a fine Adama cut (forty-five degrees) and embossed with a classic Underwood typeface: Unstoppable.

I had no idea Charre was serious. Literally serious. Literally: As my skillz grew, so did hers.

If you're a timeslip noob or a millennial boomer, you're probably lost already unless you're a cosmic groupie; in which case: Hi! How are ya?

Let me try to catch you up:

This was all back in '52. The era of cuff-rolled green jeans and Jazz Dean with his come-hither third eye. An era when PepsiUp still contained illicit spice; spirulina mini burgers had sesame seed buns, and bombshells came in two varieties. It was also the Golden Age of comix so every other immigrant landing on Elon Island for processing was quick to write in the Hero archetype to fast-track citizenship— even though only one in a thousand kept the classification after their first week's work.

We'd arrived at Earth on the ISS Hawking, folding time to make a 'slip every hour on the hour and using the snap-back to accelerate to the next fold point. (The ship was named after Steven Universe Hawking, the first AI to prove self-sentience, if you're into ships and trivia... a pretty common Ven diagram if you frequent the coastal boroughs.)

Traveling by 'slip was slow going compared to other modes but beggars can't be choosers and both Charre and I were from (different) planets that had fallen to bacterial attacks. We had to be quarantined for a year anyway so touring the Sol system seemed a good idea at the time. I think we always knew we'd settle on Earth... but let's be honest: With a global population of barely over two hundred million (only 25% native), it was one of the only planets still accepting refugees.

We'd even had choices: There'd been forty-three city-states with vacancies on the Northern continent alone when we docked in orbit, fourteen months after we'd first left our home worlds. Huddled together over a tourism tablet, Charre and I had ooed and awed at the sights, all along pretending we hadn't always known where we wanted to be. By the time we boarded a shuttle for touchdown, we were past pretense and talking openly about the lawless, contumacious, limitless possibilities of Faregrounds.

Then we switched to an immigration tablet and reality set in: In Faregrounds, we could afford a sixth floor cardboard box on First Avenue, just inside the exhaust zone of the daily shuttle. It would be a box with a private toilet and kitchenette, sure, but did we really want to asphyxiate on fumes without any of the fun side effects? And so the decision was made as the Unbuckle Your Seatbelts sign came on and an ICE officer materialized to fill the entire galley of the shuttle and block all egress. She was blue like me but thick—a Tank for sure— with black stripes iridescent like oil slicks and Charre elbowed me for staring. But I still think we got preferential treatment. Blue solidarity and all that.

We took a short-term lifetime lease on a fourth-floor walk up with solar, running water (hot and cold), a private crapper and a pretty big shower. The kitchen was smaller than the one we'd have gotten with the cardboard box but air quality was well within tolerance ranges for both our species. But we weren't in Faregrounds. Our new home was a twenty-five minute leviathan ride southwest. Statement Island.

You wouldn't know it now in 2162—a decade after our arrival—but back then the whole island was positively suburban. Nothing over ten storeys, no fast mate franchises, lots of green belt factories scrubbing the air, and quite a few swampy patches to wade through and remember home fondly. This was all before the Grosse War when the Ohmu and the Kraken Elite rearranged the face of the island, draining the swamps into the Atlantis Sea through deep impact runnels and splintering the single land mass into an uninhabitable archipelago of two dozen skerries.

Well, almost uninhabitable.

But I'm losing focus. Let's bring this back around. Back to the beginning in 2152:

Par for the course with any immigration protocol, Charre and I agreed to occupations, paid for various permits (PDA, Necessary Nudity, Houseplants), forewent others (Reproduction, Private Transport, Religious Fervor), and walked off the shuttle with a week's advance on our salaries and a lease signed in blue and purple blood. We swallowed our skillz pills and headed off with a complimentary ICE tablet that we could bake at 350 for thirty minutes after it led us to our apartment. (It tasted like chicken which neither of us had eaten before and neither of us wound up liking.)

I spent that first crossing vomiting green and yellow bile into the Narrows, overcome by the flatulent stank of the leviathan we rode on top of and wondering why the hell the Crosser couldn't chew a few alpha-galactosidase enzyme caplets and spare my (albeit sensitive) olfactory organs. In a world saved from oblivion by bioengineering, you'd think a little thing like a farting ferry boat would be easy to fix.

"Kohn? Look at the sky."

I'd been walking through the apartment, pleased even though it was still empty and considerably colder than I was used to. I went to the largest window that Charre had climbed out of ten minutes prior and frowned. "Is that safe?"

Charre just smiled, flashing all four rows of pearly sharps. "It's fused bone." She shoved the curved railing to show it didn't budge. "Some massive animal's skeleton stuck to the side of the building for emergency exodus. Recycle reuse is Earth's motto."

Once we found out it was a salvaged sperm whale ribcage we felt a little differently (the captain of the Hawking had been a Baird's beaked) but that first night we found everything about our new home endearing, quirky and charming.

I stepped out onto the bone balcony and looked up where Charre pointed a tentacle. "Oh...." Words failed me.

The canopy of night, devoid of visible stars, ruled by a single fractured moon, seemed to shimmer in waves of luminous spheres. Each one was the size of my head or a summer melon and enrobed entirely in pale pink with white spikes. From among the spikes sprouted two chitin wings, each barely extending beyond the round body of a puffer so its flight appeared comically improbable. But fly it did—they all did! There were at least a hundred of them—quite swarmy really—moving from here to there under the light bouncing off a cracked Selene.

"I love it here," Charre whispered and I looked at her. She was enraptured, enchanted.

Now it was my turn to smile. I slipped under her tentacle and she wrapped her arms around my waist, holding me from behind and resting her chin on my shoulder. "I knew you'd like it here."

"Earth is home...." She was testing out the sound and feel of it. Her body thrummed with pleasure that seeped into me through the sensory patches along my spine. "We are Earthlings."

"We are indeed." I remember feeling so content, so hopeful, so universally exactly where we were meant to be. Plus we were together. After a long distance relationship across light years, a failed marriage-and-murder on my part, and an expensively expunged criminal record on Charre's, we were finally together and ready to begin anew. Clean slate. Fresh start. All that jazz.

I didn't know then that a Mimic and a Hero would be magnets for everything seedy, underhanded and illegal… basically event horizons for the entire population of Faregrounds. Even if we did live in the suburbs.

Less than six months into our lives as Earthlings, I sat at our table made of a petrified mangrove trunk and a giant sand dollar and listened to the feed from our new social box—a gizmo that pulsed soft colors while it gave you all the news of the day in your own native tongue. Night had fallen and my shift was over; I was a daylight Hero because that's what was needed on Statement Island at the time so Charre and I worked opposite shifts (an easy mistake for a newcomer couple). Charre was getting ready for her night at the Orchid Mantis (a Faregrounds club) and I would have gone to her but the last time I tried to surprise her with a little *amour* in the shower we'd gotten tangled in the curtain beads and had to call a rescue team. Whoever invented string should be arrested and tied in knots. Just saying.

That night in particular we were the perfect example of two people who had turned their lives around. I was proud of us.

"Do you think we should get a pod?" Charre walked out of the bathroom naked and glowing a pale lavender. She smelled like salted caramel and sweet chocolate which had nothing to do with her body wash.

"Private transport? We haven't even been here a year!" Not only had we passed on getting a permit for that but even a one-seater pod would cost—

Charre flipped her backpack onto the table and winked at me

with both her inner and outer lids. Her deep purple lashes were ridiculous. I especially loved feeling them flutter against my thigh.

I opened the hook-and-loop band on her flower-shaped backpack and then stopped moving entirely. Charre had to smack me on the back to get me to breathe again. "Where did you get that much money?" I finally managed as I sucked in air like a newborn jellydog emerging from the sea.

Charre sank down into the only other chair at the table. It molded to her unique body and curled forward to cradle her tentacles so she could still motion freely with her arms and hands; Charre had started talking with her hands in the Earthling fashion that was so popular. She held them palm up and out to the side in a pose called No Big Deal. "Tips have been really good."

I just looked at her for a long quiet moment. I mean... as quiet as Statement Island ever was. We'd learned that first night half a year ago that the din from Faregrounds traveled easily across the Narrows. Cacophonous wasn't a strong enough word. It was more a discordant, asperous dissonance that waxed and waned without warning or apparent pattern and so was always present, never quite predictable white noise to be ignored. I'd wanted to buy noise canceling ear caps but with six ears the price was prohibitive. Looking again at the twenty pounds of coins in Charre's backpack, I didn't think anything would ever be cost prohibitive again!

"I had no idea flare-tending was so lucrative...." I pointedly let my words trail off as I held her gaze. To my knowledge, Charre had never lied to me before; in her home system, lying was punishable by death but we were a very, very long way from Chapprieal and the few worlds that still hosted her people.

"With two arms *and* two tentacles?" Charre lifted her thick purple eyebrows as lush as her lashes. "I can do some pretty amazing things."

I relaxed into the suggestive heat of her gaze. Tell me something I don't know about Chappriealans, right? Mixing fancy drinks and catching them on fire was child's play. Her customers should see what she could do with two arms, two tentacles, and three *sets* of genitals! (Or not. We had always been exclusive and monogamous. My failed marriage and successful murder had revolved around polygamy and I was definitely not hardwired for it.)

I touched her face, puffing my chest out like a proud something that had a chest and puffed it out when it was, you know, proud. Like a salamander, maybe. "Anything that means you won't smell like a Crosser every morning."

Charre laughed so uproariously we almost missed the coyote boys warning us of the stranger.

Are you lost again? I'm trying really hard to keep the storyline linear and straightforward but you've probably already noticed that there wasn't much straight about me and Charre. We were arguably as crooked as creatures come in terms of twisting and turning our bodies and minds into whatever we needed them to be to survive.

As a Hero, I was the face of aid and justice for ten hours every day, drifting silently through my assigned neighborhood, five square miles of personal terrain where it was up to me to maintain order for every living thing. Sometimes I called in salvage crews to remove ancient warheads from the shoreline. Other times I floated up into the highest boughs of willow trees to retrieve pet hamsters. And still more times, I was snapping the neck of an abusive spouse or a rabid arachniorse. When on shift, Heroes were connected to the Authority Intelligence (what AI had become) so I was officer, jury, and executioner. On shift, I could think in 120 FPS while the AI judge (which was really a global network) could instruct me in nanoseconds so there was no lag.

When I was on shift. Only on shift. Off the clock, I processed information like any other Hunte and I certainly couldn't drift or float or neutralize a fueled up junkie or cracked out attacker. I'm mentioning all this because I need you to know that, legally, I wasn't a Hero when it all happened. Charre's skillz pill had put thousands of drink routines in her mind and muscles and she had memorized dozens of them on her own so she could whip us up a pair of Flaming Flamingos or Birthday Cake Martinis but my skillz were not accessible to me after work hours.

Someone collapsed hard against our front door. Which was also our only door. Someone... or something.

I don't want to lie and say we both jumped up and ran to investigate. Or that my Hero skillz kicked in or activated after hours somehow and I was driven to help. The truth is: We just sat there for another moment or three. We looked at each other and spoke soundlessly in that way that certain couples have. Neither of our species are telepathic but Charre and I have an emotional shorthand of glances and expressions, a silent language of our bodies that speaks volumes along the channel of our private connection.

We went toward the sound together.

When the curvy human woman with her moonlight skin and platinum blonde coif tumbled unconscious over our threshold, we realized our door had been the only thing holding her up. We also realized our lives would change forever. Again.

We'd been Earthlings for less than a year but even we knew of the meteoric climb to fame, activism, and sex appeal of media star Marilyn Molone.

Charre took a "sick day." A old hold over from when the planet was majority populated with humans and their shitty immune systems that were further compromised by deadly cocktails of genetic errors—specifically the double shot of competitive and hierarchal behavior often called the Octavia Principle after the scholar who wrote the thesis.

It was more likely that Charre or I would sprout puffer wings and fly across the sky on the night of the full moon than we'd be unable to work due to some microbial germ. It was an unexpected and high-toll benefit of coming from worlds conquered by the Brine. Survivors received free treatment from the Intergalactic Alliance of Systems that made us immune to all common bacteria and viruses alike. But a survivor's toll wasn't just emotional; the treatment was expensive—we'd be paying the Alliance a tithe until the day we died. The Alliance didn't want their greatest enemy to spread through the universe and their pacifist policies didn't allow them to euthanize exposed survivors. Between me and Charre, millions of Brine had probably been killed during our antiviral treatment. But the Alliance didn't see Brine as alive. Long story short: Charre could stay home without penalty and neither of us were afraid when Marilyn finally awoke and announced, "The Brine are trying to kill me."

At that point I had several instantaneous questions: Where is your security detail? Why did you come to us of all people? Have you been exposed already? Have you contacted the Alliance for treatment? Does anyone else know the Brine are on Earth?!

But Charre spoke first: "How do you know their motives?"

Leave it to Charre to cut through the emotional baggage and cultural niceties to the nitty, gritty, bloody blue heart of the matter.

Marilyn sat up slowly. She wasn't very tall and looked especially fragile curled up in the corner of our inflatable couch. I felt bad because we'd had relatively ruckus sex on that couch just yesterday night and I hadn't gotten around to cleaning it yet. We'd slipped off her high heels so as not to risk puncturing our furniture and her nylon-covered feet stuck to the upholstery a little. Oops.

She drew her cream-colored, long-haired jacket more tightly around her. I think it was made of gold skultula silk or maybe dyed borzoi but when we'd moved her to the couch the jacket had felt softer than anything I'd ever worn, that's for sure.

"I'm a biological physicist," Marilyn told us carefully. "My life's work is trying to establish communication with the Brine. My name is—"

"—Marilyn Molone." I finished her sentence for her and looked from her wary, exhausted face to Charre. Charre's eyes were narrowed and she was staring at the woman with what looked like intense scrutiny.

"You know me?" The desperate hope on Marilyn's face was almost too much.

"You're…" Charre began slowly. "…a media star and activist for human rights."

The smallest bit of color that had crept into Marilyn's fair cheeks drained away. She bowed her head, curling into her jacket as if searching for comfort that we obviously weren't providing.

"You don't know me," she whispered, more to herself, I think, than to us.

Charre blinked all her lids and looked at me. I let my confusion show on my face and felt a cold chill even though it was only early autumn and the windows were closed against the distant din of Faregrounds.

"You… *look* like you," I offered lamely. What did I know of comforting human women? Even as a Hero, I rescued, retrieved, and recycled all numbers of species but it was all accomplished with a certain level of detachment. Plus, I'll say it again: I wasn't on duty so my skillz slumbered.

Marilyn plucked at the soft spider silk or fur of her jacket that most likely cost more than the entire brownstone we lived in. I felt pretty certain I'd seen photos on the feed of her wearing that very same gold-and-cream wrap.

"When I came to this morning..." She was whispering again. "...I was nude."

Then she looked up at us. She looked truly at us as if for the first time.

"Where I come from," her voice was very strong for someone who had apparently been unconscious more than once today. "Aliens don't exist."

And that's how we knew that the Marilyn Molone who sat on our sticky couch, in our working class walk-up on Statement Island was not the Marilyn Molone who lived in the Venus Penthouse, made movies in Sky City, and advocated for human-only spaces. No, this bombshell (and she was very beautiful, seemingly identical in every physical way) was from a world, timeline, dimension, alternate reality where it was still okay to call someone an alien to their face.

Infinite variations. It's a misleading phrase. Or maybe just an ignorant one. Though it seems pretty judgmental to call something ignorant just because it's archaic. If "infinite variations" was the best they knew, who are we to disparage them?

I can imagine Charre's toothy smile even now. There would be love and tenderness on her face as she flashed her array of sharps. She'd learned early in our relationship that I had a fascination with parallel worlds and she'd known pretty much from that first night that I had a soft spot for Marilyn in particular. I honestly don't know whether it was her wide, deep blue eyes spaced far apart in her face, or her white-blonde waves of collar-length hair, or even the little mark of beauty to the side of her full lips, but whatever it was, I wanted to protect her. I wanted to believe her. I didn't want to be an alien... I wanted to be an ally.

So we learned that the dimensional possibilities only extended as far as was probable for a single entity—one world for every shade of gray. And those were planes above our own. Whereas the manifestations that were opposite and opposing, lay in under-planes below our own. And every entity on every plane influenced the possibilities above and below.

I think it's most accurate to say: Parallel worlds exist as beautiful gradients each bleeding into one another with influence but without mutual awareness.

Now that I stop and think about it, I suppose that seems pretty close to infinite but it's a gradual infinity; the most disparate shades were so far apart they might as well not exist in one another's reality.

Do I sound like a biological physicist yet? In our world, we had known Marilyn Molone no more than as a talented, passionate actor who wanted to carve out safe havens for her dying people. But in her world—"her" meaning the Marilyn that collapsed against our door that night—we were Charlotte and John Rubicon, childhood friends who had supported her rise in the emerging study of microbial life forms.

Flash forward ten years and our Marilyn (who wasn't *ours* at all) would be dead and *their* Marilyn (who we'd grown to love) had returned to her world with a mind so full of cosmic truths she would hold the highest office of her nation for not one but four terms.

We'd come to Earth and everything had changed. The trajectory of our shared destiny—what Charre and I were meant to be and do. Charre was a Mimic now. She knew how to blend in and make people feel comfortable around her, want to be with her. And I was a Hero. Skillz on or off, I was meant to help.

Our apartment became a lighthouse. A beacon across the

broken island after the war and a haven long before that across dimensions. Marilyn was the first but far from the last and our lives grew fuller, more complicated, more dangerous and mysterious and wondrous with each new traveler we encountered.

What did you do today?

Lost in Translation

There is a quality to light as it passes through a population of dust that is mesmerizing even in the worst of moments. The way the white-gold winter sun, the pale sun of a dying year, enrobes each particle and transforms it into something more than entropy, something more than the aftermath of a world war still inundating the trade winds, into something divine yet fleeting, momentary but irrevocably worth watching, worth admiring, and perhaps, in rare, horrendous and unprecedented moments— sometimes—worth possessing.

I'm jealous of dust. It's unencumbered by the new world order. Free to move and exist as it is. I'm jealous of the seven and a half billion of my kind who are nothing now but dust themselves. Never before have I been jealous of the dead.

Your delivery was delayed.

My palms are flat against the hardwood floor. Dust settles between my fingers. I am kneeling in a pool of sunlight. I am kneeling in the cinders of our dead.

Were you ill?

My pounding heart threatens to break through my breastbone and tumble, still throbbing, into my lap. I imagine impossible horrors like this far too frequently since I saw our world fall impossibly fast. As far as I know, they don't get sick. The idea of a faulty immune system amuses them.

My mouth chooses self-preservation over the fear trying to choke me: "I wasn't ill, *Gi'sye.*" As instructed by Director Anarode at the San Francisco Alignment Center, I use the *Gibtre'hon* equivalent for 'Commander.' A designation in their complex society where cultural, spiritual, political and martial are all interwoven. I know how lucky I am to be here instead of in a classroom, in a zoo, or on a laboratory table.

I also know that my owner—like all *Gibtre'hon*—is long and slender, a will-of-the-wisp stretched tall, with a penchant for 'collecting' the exotic and unique. My stress-induced weight-loss was corrected—aggressively—as soon as I was purchased. The intravenous feeds had burned through me like napalm in my veins.

Good.

It's not time to look up. I was hooded during transport because they insist we stay calmer when we see less. I don't mind the blinders; they make sense. I'm not sure I'd still be sane if I saw everything there was to see. But ignorance is not bliss: I know what we crushed in the road on the way here today, what the spiked treads of the leviathan ground into an Earth that was no longer ours.

Burning bodies is wasteful, I'd heard Director Anarode say once. *Healthy bodies can be consumed.* Meaning: Not by them; they were vegan. *The tainted can be turned into the soil with terraforming microbes to—*

I'd tuned out or blocked out the rest. Some of those tainted bodies had been my friends, my family, my wife, my son.

Do you have a name?

I wonder, for just an instant, how long I can stay silent. How long can I *not* answer a direct question? I consider counting the seconds but before I reach 'two' my mouth is already moving, "My name is whatever you wish, *Gi'sye*."

I sense… pleasure. Or approval? They don't make wordless sounds like 'oh' or 'hm' to express raw emotions as is—as was—so common with humans. They project their emotions, containing not so much a tone of voice as a breadth and depth of diapason. These projections lace *between* their words. In short: My owner is pleased I'm so well-trained.

I wish to know your human name.

The words are not spoken. They are not shared aloud the way we speak. They are broadcast in some type of waveform that thrums against our ear drums while leaving the room silent. Something about the neuroimplants they bored into our heads.

Almost imperceptibly, my hands shake. The hardwood floor is polished oak. Polished by generations of humans coming and going from this room once occupied by a Silicon Valley billionaire; how interesting that the ascetics of the American one-percent match the ascetics of our executioners. How apropos.

Despite my conditioning, despite my now-intrinsic (now-biological?) fear of pain, I hold off answering. I know the *Gibtre'hon* sometimes find our names challenging. I don't want to—

First my neck warms beneath my wide silicone collar then my face tingles. This will be my only warning. I answer, "Renae."

Ree-Nuh.

"Ree-Nay." Oh my god. What have I done? My adrenaline spikes. I hear my blood in my ears, feel it in my cheeks. Was my indoctrination too efficient or not efficient enough? Despite not being asked a direct question, I spoke. Is my will even my own?

There is palpable tension after my unsolicited correction. A tangible silence in the golden oak and cold white room. My owner makes no sound whatsoever but the feeling of consideration, of contemplation, is as obvious as the shaft of light I continue to kneel in, as obvious as the eddies of dust dancing away each time I exhale.

The *Gibtre'hon* are so much more than we ever were. Our superiors—faster, smarter, stronger. They exist in twice as many dimensions, or rather, they are aware of and can perceive and manipulate six as opposed to three. They are space-faring. They are genderless. They have evolved beyond petty, compulsive, imprecise violence to decisive, savage deconstruction in veneration of the scientific method. Every act they commit is in pursuit of *Jyhor*—their Divine State of Knowing.

Theirs is a deadly intellect.

Renae.

Said perfectly this time but also without an emotional footnote which is rare for their people. I hold my breath. My eyes sink shut in my bowed face. Without context, lost in the stillness of despondency, I am blind to what comes next. I've spent the last year behind the walls of the Center. I have never been owned before.

I shall call you Nuufi.

A part of me dies. Another part. I had no idea before our end that we had so many parts capable of death. It's incredible really that our bodies persist. Is this the truth behind the old human fascination with zombies and the undead? Because we knew our bodies would persevere even when our hearts and minds screamed for release. Why ask my name at all?

My eyes open with the realization: To take it away from me.

My conditioning continues even now.

Do you know what it means?

I shake my head slowly and feel no shame as tears spill from my eyes. I remember they like it when we nod and shake our heads because they value sight over sound. I hate myself when I please them but it's hard not to. I'm alive—even if only partially—because I please them.

It means: Brave and foolish in equal measure.

My turn to be stunned. I remain quiet. My tears stop. Their language is, arguably, as beautiful as they are. Some called them angels when they first arrived. Ethereal creatures resonating in place... in many places all at the same time. We had no chance.

Say it.

I inhale, drawing remnants of our civilization as loess into my lungs, into my body where it will be no safer, and no more alive, than it was floating in this room or resting between my fingers on the floor. I want to think I swallowed courage or resistance or something that made me defy that direct order but, honestly, I think I was just wearing down, trembling more, exhausting my energy at the end of this seemingly endless day.

My collar activates and my body jolts, seizing in response to the web of pain slicing across my face. My optical nerves cease to send messages to my brain and I fight to stay upright. I fight to stay conscious. I feel my lips curl back, my eyes bulge, straining from their sockets, blood trickling from my nose. The contortions feel like they're pulling my face apart; that's where they strike us, disfigure us. Our faces are our identity and they learned it too quickly. They wanted us to be the numbers on our collars; numbers that were *Gibtre'hon*, not even human.

The pain stops. My breathing is labored. My sight returns. Bare feet stand before me. Bare legs. Both are longer, thinner than the human counterparts. Six toes and countless bones beneath skin the color of eggplant or slate with indigo highlights almost invisible to the naked eye. And those bones? Not quite like ours. They shifted and moved in ways unfamiliar and unfettered. A sheer sash—the color of almost-translucent buttercream—brushes the crown of my head.

When at war, the *Gi'sye* wore wine red. But the war was over and antique eggshell was their color of victory.

Look at me.

I do.

I want to.

But I'm also willed to.

I am Helahna Fahrour. You will call me Gi'sye.

Her full, dark plum lips did not move. Their mouths never moved when they spoke. Her eyes are glossy black and especially wide without white sclera or visible iris. She has lashes like raven feathers and indigo patterns move over her skin in concentric circles as if she created Venn diagrams of every situation, determining each possible course of action. She isn't smiling. They don't have facial expressions as far as I know.

Wait.

I pause. I blink.

Why did I use a pronoun?

Say it.

I want to shout, to scream, to rage against the dying of my own kind that my name was and would forever be Renae Riley Williamson. But instead I value my life over my pride and answer, "Nuufi."

There was pleasure in the room between us and some of it, I won't lie, was mine. Me looking up at her—so far to her face, easily seven feet above my sublimate position—and her looking down. She is pleased because I said my new name. I am pleased because looking at them produces cortisol and dopamine in the human body. This was true even before I was collared and implanted for an owner. Is my reaction to her more intense because I am her possession?

Good, she tells me. But what I hear, what the underlying

emotion laces into and around the word, is: *Good girl.*

I think to myself: Do I get a treat?

It is October 25, 2021. Somewhere near 7:30 in the morning and the sun is rising. My owner would say this moment is 1.225 AGA, one orbital rotation plus 225 axial rotations After *Gibtre'hon* Arrival.

They call this Earth Local Time as opposed to *Gibtre'hon* Universal Time which is expressed as a multidimensional glyph incomprehensible to human eyes that see only in two dimensions. They find this amusing. How biologically primitive we are. How simple.

We make wonderful pets.

I am not allowed a clock or books or tools with which to write. There's apparently no reason for us to track time as we exist only within the schedule of our owner's. Likewise, we cannot create anything recognizable as worthy so why would we need pencil or paper? *Written language is imperfect*, Director Anarode often said.

I was given my own room but this isn't uncommon. I learned from the ever-informative Anarode that, while not *Gi'sye*, as the Director of an Alignment Center, he had jurisdiction over the thousand human charges interred there. Though in my twelve months at the Center I never once saw another human face or heard another human sound. Again: The blinder method at work.

I could have lain in my room, unable to sleep, obediently prone on my back staring at the off-white blank canvas of the ceiling and engaged my brain with an interior dialogue about why I thought of Anarode as male and my owner as female. Their bodies were configured alike beneath their conventional sashes: Smooth, flat chests, narrow hips, devoid of navels or genitalia. (Though Anarode's body was coral pink and sherbet orange with angler bronze lines.) Their sashes were both *Gibtre'hon* living fabric fortified with cybernetic threads that pulsed with faint color, both worn draped behind the neck and across the front of the shoulders and chest, falling to mid-thigh and never seeming to slide or askew. (Though Anarode's seemed less sheer, less luxurious, and was pale blue like the rest of the Center staff.)

Instead, I lay on my molded platform, the semi-malleable block not unlike firm gelatin, wracked with waves of cold from a new realization: They exist everywhere. They have AGA dates on planets throughout the universe.

After *Gibtre'hon* Arrival.

Nuufi.

I awaken when I hear my name so I must have fallen asleep. I sit up on my block, blinking and touching my face like a child. She stands in the open doorway of my room. Always open as it has no door, not even indentations where hinges once were. "Yes, Helahna?"

Oh my god. I'm half asleep. I'm poorly adjusting to life outside the Center. Is it a Freudian malfunction? My wife's name was Hannah. Is it Stockholm Syndrome? My face twitches anticipating the punishment of pain. I can't breathe.

I don't recall closing my eyes but my sleeping block agitates and when I open my eyes, Helahna is sitting there looking at me.

We look at each other.

She blinks slowly, deliberately. *You are... unexpected.*

Before the end of days, before humans fell, I worked and thrived as a professor of psychology at Stanford. Is this why my life was spared? Or was it just my emerald green eyes, my rich, dark skin and my fine straight hair like black spider's silk? I catalog every tiny nuance of her, memorizing and categorizing, classifying her as best I can try to understand. This is contemplation of the unexpected, that slow blink. As close to an expression as I've ever seen.

"I can't imagine you find anything unexpected, *Gi'sye,*" I hear

130

myself whisper perhaps because I don't have the courage for more. "After all, *Nuufi* means brave and foolish in equal measure."

She does not smile. She does not grin. She does not tilt her head or blush or hum softly. I miss those small sensory cues that humans once exchanged in intimate moments of connection. Nonetheless, I sense an intimacy—somehow—between us.

You are a fast learner. Again: Pleasure. I'm worth what I cost, apparently.

She stands then and crosses the room, her back to me without hesitance because they all know we can't harm them once we've been implanted and trained; it's physiologically impossible. I study her bare back. They have more vertebrae. Can they turn their heads like sloths and owls? I shudder.

I think our interaction is over when she passes through my doorway and starts down the hall but even as I look down, considering everything that has transpired, she turns back and faces me.

Nuufi, do you want a companion?

Yes! I want to jump up and shout it through laughter. I know my eyes widen in shock and delight and hope. A hundred times: Yes!

But then realization. It was just a moment. Just a small lapse in control and composure and judgment. Don't give her something else to take away, I tell myself. Your thoughts are still your own, I remind myself. Don't give in, I command myself.

"Whatever you think is best, *Gi'sye*," I say almost instantly. But I'm not ignorant. I know she saw every emotion that flashed across my face. Despite it, she projects satisfaction and turns once more to leave. "*Gi'sye?*" What am I doing?!

She stops and her surprise washes over me but it's a charmed surprise, a welcome one. *What is it, Nuufi?*

I wet my lips, suddenly dry even though it's impossible for me to be dehydrated when my sleeping block seeps moisture and nutrients into my body. "Did you want something? You… came to my door."

She doesn't have to want something. She has every right to stand in my doorway and say my name. Or have me kneel for hours. Or trade me in. Or beat me senseless. I'm hers.

I wanted your presence.

And there it is. My mistake. My fatal operating error. It's there woven between the words. *Her companionship should be enough.* I am suddenly afraid I have ruined everything… but what is 'everything?' What does 'everything' mean and how is my life as it is now not completely and utterly ruinous already?

Nuufi.

I look up. Again, I was unaware I'd looked away. My physical responses are elicited before my knowledge of them as if responding to her is autonomic.

Her large black eyes are like midnight skies.

I prefer it when you call me Helahna.

She leaves my doorway completely then, soundless as always, but the projection of emotion lingers in the room. The feeling is subtle, soft and sad. A mixture of understanding, patience and sorrow.

"Whatever you wish," I exhale beneath a breath and I know with certainty that no matter where she is in this massive complex of chrome, glass, oak and off-white walls, she hears me.

My internal clock—or one of the six implants in my brain—wakes me at sunrise every day after that and I have no need to ever wash or eat. The gelatinous block takes care of my necessities but when Helahna finds me curled one day in the over-stuffed nest-like chair in her living room tugging at tangles in my hair? An hour later she appears with a rolled cloth, climbs into the nest and sinks down behind me.

I have no idea what's about to happen but I sense it's best to stay still. She unrolls the cloth beside us and I almost laugh aloud with relief. A matching comb and brush inlaid with Mother of Pearl. Nail clippers. An emery board. Thinning sheers. Helahna has purchased a human grooming kit.

For the next hour, the alien Commander who slaughtered my people, brushes my hair until I almost fall asleep.

Today, your companion arrives.

She says this when she finally rises, taking her kit with her. It has been seven or eight days since she offered in my doorway. I have thought about that moment, replaying it over and over a great many times but I have never dared make an inquiry. It seemed safer to consider it all a dream.

As she starts to walk away, I catch her hand.

And my collar activates.

It activates like never before. My hands fly to my face as it threatens to peel away from the front of my skull. I scream, thrash, writhe. My eyes bleed; I smear bright red blood all over the buttercream furniture.

No. Not on the nest. Helahna is holding me, firmly, protectively, and the buttercream splattered with blood is her victory sash. I look up at her face and she opens her mouth.

Her teeth are steel or titanium or something silver and so sharp they literally glint in the soft light of the room. Before I can catch my breath to scream anew, she strikes, ripping my collar off with her razor teeth.

It is seven hours later. Helahna carried me to my room, laid me on my block. I slept but I'm relatively certain it was induced. Several times I awoke to Anarode in the room, holding a new collar, and I thought I was back at the Center and I started to weep like a little child.

Nuufi, Nuufi.

Helahna is there. Comforting me. Telling me, not with her words, but with the emotions between the words that I am home. That my home is there with her. That she will not return me to the Center.

And there's something more as well. Helahna is... angry. Not angry at me. Angry at Anarode.

At one point I wake and they're facing each other, maybe two inches apart, and Helahna is seething. Her fury is so protective of me and so directed at Anarode that I feel respected, honored, safe. I know she could very well be complaining about faulty merchandise but as I sink back into unconsciousness—into healing?—she glances at me and I know she isn't complaining.

For the first time, I touch my neck. My skin is unbroken and my neck is bare. My collar is gone and has not been replaced. Nor will it be. Inexplicably, I dream of fields of red poppies being eaten by a colony of black rabbits. Their eyes are ringed in white like expensive eyeliner and their teeth are tiny silver knives.

When next I wake it's deep into the night and the director of the Center is thankfully gone. One wall of my room is windows that overlook the Santa Cruz Mountains but right now they lie beneath the cloak of night only sparsely dotted with the distant lights from the homes of other Commanders; I am not certain that the *Gibtre'hon* sleep.

I sit up very slowly and my entire body aches but it is my face that burns like how I imagine an expensive chemical peal would feel the day after. I reach up with both hands but Helahna is with me—perhaps always has been—and takes my hands between her own.

You will heal. You will not scar.

But though her touch and words are comforting, are laced with affection and even a thin trace of apology, I cringe and cower, only her firm grip on my hands stops me from pulling away. My implants and conditioning still hold even without the interface of the collar.

Helahna lets go and we look at each other. Without words, she stands from my block and walks to my doorway. Only there does she turn and speak to me—more information than any of her kind have ever shared in all my days as theirs.

Your collar was too finely calibrated. Most of us do not want the unsolicited touch of a human. But I am not afraid of humans.

Oh the volumes behind her words! The inflections and truths and excerpts from her rage against Anarode. She is *Gi'sye!* A Commander! Revered among her people. A veteran of countless 'arrivals' on alien worlds. A collector of beautiful things.

I don't speak. I only listen, allowing the myriad facets of her language to inform, horrify and enlighten me.

I will not collar you again. You are free to touch me as you please. I know you will not harm me and I am not xenophobic. I...

I'm speechless. If I had wanted to speak I wouldn't have had the words. Never had I heard a *Gibtre'hon* stumble or hesitate like this.

...I trust you, Nuufi.

I catch my breath and realize I've been holding it. In that moment, with the golden warm light of the house haloing Helahna's body, illuminating her sash, I admit she does look angelic. If I am equally brave and foolish, then she is equally Grim Reaper and savior.

I will let you heal.

She projects calm and I return the favor by being ungrateful and callus: "Did my companion arrive?"

Helahna projects nothing. There is an absence of emotion or

undercurrent. I realize she can hide from me. Would that be useful somehow? Useful for what? Useful how and to what ends? Was the end game simply to understand our conquerors?

If she had participated in the occupation of numerous worlds, that assumed she eventually left them as she certainly wasn't on them now. Would Helahna someday leave Earth? Would all the *Gibtre'hon* leave?!

I will fetch him.

She left me to contemplate not her rare use of a gender pronoun but a dozen other emotions and considerations warring for my attention.

A few minutes later I'm sitting akimbo on my block with nervous butterflies in my stomach like a child. I had tried to focus on the gift of information Helahna had given me but even two or three minutes in I felt light-headed and overwhelmed. Whatever the collar had done to me it was taking all the *Gibtre'hon* tech inside me to fix it.

The golden puppy that bounded across the floor was the definition of unexpected. He spotted me instantly even in the nighttime room and promptly peed himself in excitement. Had it been nineteen months since he'd seen a human? Could he even be that old? Imagine being domesticated by a species only for it to vanish!

I was holding him, cooing to him, burying my face in his silken fur when Helahna returned to stand in the doorway. She watched me for sometime and I pretended not to notice because I just wanted to lose myself in this moment for just a little longer... a few weeks or years perhaps.

I am confident you approve of your companion.

The puppy jolted as if shocked with electricity. He leapt at me, pawing, clumsy, squealing, trying to burrow under me, shaking his head so violently he would have thrown himself from the sleeping block had I not held him tighter.

Helahna projected confusion and I lifted my face to her to, hopefully, show that I was in the same state she was.

"It's okay, boy. It's okay. It's—" I just repeated the useless phrase over and over again because I was easily as helpless (and almost as clueless) as the dog was. Eventually he calmed into a low, pitiful whining, shoving his fat, fluffy puppy body into the bowl of my crisscrossed legs.

I shrugged for Helahna and hoped she'd like a shrug the way she liked nods and head shakes. "Thank you." I tried to weave sincerity into the words and for the first time I felt like I understood why humans seemed so rudimentary to *Gibtre'hon*. Our language was so limited!

You are welcome—

But she didn't finish because the sounds of the puppy howling, barking, crying and moaning filled the room—most likely the entire house! Staying with the theme of nervous butterflies, I gasped as I made the guess, "I think... your voice is hurting him." Tread carefully, I admonished myself, unconsciously holding the dog even tighter. "The special frequency of a *Gibtre'hon* voice... it may be painful to dogs."

I poured everything into those two sentences. All the gratitude I felt toward Helahna for not returning me to the Center. All the gratitude I felt for the gift of the puppy. I wanted—I needed—her to know that I was not complaining. She had given me so many gifts.

And it worked. Because she gave me another: She stayed silent and bobbed her head once in acknowledgement in a way her people never do. She projected—without words—into the room: Understanding. Patience. And an assurance that everything would be all right. She would make sure it was all right.

Just as quietly then she took her leave. I cleaned up the mess on the floor with toilet paper from the small quarter bath attached to my room then climbed back on the block and curled around Lucky who was already sleeping as deeply as only puppies can sleep.

When I awoke the next morning at sunrise, Lucky was gone.

I wept. I wept like I hadn't in all the days since the *Gibtre'hon* destroyed almost everyone and everything. I wept for everything and everyone I'd known. Because I wasn't drowning in fear—for once, for the first time since it all began—the grief welled up from deep inside me and rose like a tsunami to drown me.

I'm not entirely certain when Helahna entered my room. But when she sat down on the block beside me and gathered me into her arms I was drenched in tears and snot and making sounds that weren't anywhere near words. I was as primal and primitive as possible, broken down completely and unable to function except to cry harder.

And yet....

A not-so-small part of me wanted to rage against her, pound my fists into her, break her unbreakable bones. The games she played! The twisted and vile manipulations! Was I not subservient enough? Was I not exactly what I was conditioned by her people to be?!

Perhaps it was part of that conditioning that stopped me from doing everything—anything—violent or aggressive. But in my mind it was Helahna's words in my head, deep in my ears: *I trust you.*

Even if I would not—could not—trust Helahna, I would not turnabout that unfair play. I would hold the moral high ground as if it were my last stand. This was the only thing I could—

Lucky bounded into the room.

Lucky leapt onto the block.

Lucky licked sorrow from my face.

He will no longer dysfunction, Helahna told me with humor and amusement between her words as Lucky nuzzled her hand then chased the edge of her sash.

He did not react to her voice. He didn't cringe or yelp or cower. He never would again. Because he would never hear anything again.

Gi'sye Helahna Fahrour had had his entire auditory system removed and grafted over with precision. His ears were completely cosmetic now, like custom pieces perched on his head, leading nowhere, doing nothing.

Today, I will introduce you to the rest of my household, Helahna told me. *They have given you space at my bequest but they grow eager to meet you.*

I could not look at her. I felt cold. The air felt thin.

They changed everything to fit them.

She stood and walked to my doorway. My guardian. My jailer. My owner.

I think you will fit in perfectly, Nuufi. A wonderful addition to my collection.

Terms of Service

By this point in the journey, I'm too self-aware to give myself over to inspiration. My brain has caught up with my hands; a forty-six year relay race of psychological proportions that I've only recently realized twenty years of therapy only made worse. (Though, most likely, kept me alive and out of jail.)

A storm has blown in from over the ocean and stalled above us, caught between the Olympic and Cascade mountains, an armada of bumper car clouds rigged for thunder, lightning, and brief downpours with every hapless collision. Sitting down to write, the house is quiet in a way it rarely is; with the power out, the absence of hum and buzz is almost a sound in and of itself. The voice of modern life silenced to remind me, needlessly, of the true necessities.

"We could walk away," you whisper to me one night. "Just you and me and the kids. Just vanish into the world. Explore."

And I hold you tighter and understand every place those words are coming from and how incredibly close we've been to exactly that on too many occasions than I care to count.

I make love to you that night and you fall asleep afterward with your head on my shoulder.

I think about the couples who sleep in separate rooms, different beds, facing away from each other on opposite sides of the mattress. Why are all those practices more believable than dreaming intertwined? I didn't wait for you until I was deep into my thirties to sleep alone.

A scarlet candle burns in an iron lantern fit with bubbled panes, the flame flickering behind the raindrops suspended in the glass. Small creatures of shadow and light move like the souls of Flatlanders across my notebook page and my pen is still, soundless while I watch them. I feel like any moment one of them will reach out a slender tendril to touch the quivering black pearl of ink glistening in the candle light.

If I set my pen aside slowly, if I move with greatest care, would I be able to hold one of these shades trying to make my page their own?

I look at my hands. They are finally the hands I wanted when I was a little girl: Small, square, blue veins nestled between tendons, nails rounded and short, capable. The soft layers of youth no longer pad these tools of my trade, of pretty much every trade I've ever engaged in.

Even when I was seven, I wanted the hands of a forty year old.

Tonight, beneath the storm and a house of sleeping animals and children, I feel a cold thread of frustration. I am focused on the shadow play of the lantern because the black and white of pen and page are not cooperating, my bidding be damned. This is rare and unexpected, unheard of. I have made a life of my body doing as told, when told. I make the demands. I set the rules. Hunger, exhaustion, desire, fury: All on schedule, all premeditated and certainly under control.

I don't want to write nonfiction. I want to be remembered by what I create, not by what created me.

My mother always pushed me toward nonfiction. And my paternal grandmother. And my first and only professor.

"*This* story," said dyke memoirist Rebecca Brown, holding up my story *Modern Fabrics*—published now in sixteen languages and thirty publications—in front of the adult students in her University of Washington Creative Writing class. "Doesn't even feel like it was written by the person who wrote *this* story." And she waves the science fiction fable I turned in that week. "Stick to nonfiction, DiMarco."

And I sat in silence. Seventeen years old. Younger by a decade or three than anyone else in the room. Allowed to attend by special permission from the head of the department. Angry. Embarrassed. And confused: One week earlier, I'd received an offer from a New York publishing house for my science fiction trilogy.

I had taken the class because I wanted to keep learning the craft I loved, high school was done, and college wasn't in the cards. Carol Pearl. Sandra Whaley. Eleanor Weston. I was looking for a new teacher and mentor. Rebecca's bio in the instructor directory mentioned her published works: *The Terrible Girls* and *The Haunted House*. I assumed she wrote children's books or Nancy Drew-adjacent adventures. (This was before the era of search engines, back when dial up AOL was revolutionary.)

Instead, I walked in on Day One and she stabbed a cantaloupe with a pen knife, ripped it open like bone and flesh, and ate it with her hands and face like an animal. She didn't wipe her mouth before she assigned, "That's your writing prompt. Fifteen minutes. Write!" My first experience with a shock jock, a kind of Camille Paglia/Pacific Northwest feminist lesbian hybrid.

Between useless *bon mots* harvested from her life (a life devoid of *Writing Down the Bones* or *The Elements of Style* apparently), she repeatedly complained about how the Lammys always overlooked her. (She won a year later for her AIDS hospice book.) I don't think anyone else in the room even knew what the Lambda Awards were and I couldn't have cared less she felt slighted; the only time I was more disappointed to discover my professor was a self-marginalized (my homage to May Sarton) gay author was the year I received a broken pogo stick for Christmas.

I attended only half the sessions I paid for then left for a two-year national book tour with my science fiction bestseller.

Lightning outside the window or the flash of errant headlights through ten acres of trees? Isn't it too cold in November for lightning? Does lightning have a season?

I think about the first time I saw purple lightning. I think about the second time. Both times I had a woman beneath me. Both times she was far more dangerous than the lightning. I had a twenty year season where toxic women were the only women I wanted to fuck. The worse they treated me, the more I wanted to hear them scream my name.

"How about you make *me* say your name," you propose one night, your gaze heated and your kisses Coke-a-Cola sweet. "Aren't I more deserving?"

And you did more with a dozen words than twice-a-week therapy ever did.

I want to hear something. The quiet of the house is disconcerting me. I unbar and unlock the sliding window beside my desk. The orchard trees bend low in reverence. Their branches are bare of cherries, apples, and magnolia blooms bigger than my head (and I have a pretty big head). The arbor creaks in discordance, held together mostly by the twenty-year-old grape vines that harden into stone snakes every winter, petrified until springtime breeches their hulls from within.

Dangling by yarn from the ceiling, skeleton keys my father left behind. Some of them are stamped with digits: 2B, 7. None of them yield their mysteries.

He died long before his forties. A year younger than my mother, so only twenty when I was born. Threatened, terrorized and finally killed at the hands of corrupt police when I was four years old and my sister was T-minus two months. I have students older than he lived to be. I have a son almost his final age.

Because he trusted the wrong people. Because he lived before mental health care had caught up to his needs. Because creative, long-haired, effeminate men don't last as long as the brutal, demeaning savages that all too often populate positions of power.

I close the window again. I don't want the storm to get in.

I grew up with two moms. So the last thing I go looking for in my life are lesbians. Like every other red-blooded American teen, to break away from my parents, to become an adult, I craved the opposite and dreaded the familiar. They always seemed driven by finances, budgets, the next "get rich" scheme, so I dove into philanthropy and raised my children to value living on less. It wasn't living paycheck to paycheck, it was living without a paycheck all together.

It helped that my biological mother was the other reason I hated nonfiction. She was far less subtle than my bulldozer professor. Having been a published poet of deeply personal reflection before I was born, my mother's preference for nonfiction was as obvious as her sexuality (worn on her sleeve until my sister came out as bisexual and our mother announced she was too). It didn't help that I attended an alternate high school focused on the arts and every contest—

PNWC, Bumbershoot, Cascadia, Outlook—I entered for extra credit I won. With nonfiction.

What parent pushes their child *away* from kudos?

"You can stock shelves or be night janitors," I tell my children all their lives. "You can be doctors or lawyers or teachers or chefs. But whatever you are, be happy. Have work or have a home you return to every night that makes you content."

Contentment is not money. I know far too many wealthy people who are intrinsically, deeply, irrevocably, discontent. Money can solve problems. Money can make life easier. But life can be wondrous even full of problems and hardships.

"What are you writing tonight?" You smile at me, wrapping your arms around my shoulders from behind. You entered my study soundlessly even in our soundless home. You take up so little room, demand so little space, I often think of you as simply smaller than me despite your extra inches. Your skin smells like lavender, your cheek softer than satin against the line of my jaw.

"Fiction," I say. An old joke that always makes you smile. You know my life better than anyone else.

You lean into the dancing light, read my sparse page and ask, "What part is fiction?"

You're still smiling and in such close proximity I sink into your natural bouquet. Lavender and cinnamon and something like cardamom or jasmine. A mix of candles and incense and whatever you smoked while you built a fire earlier this evening. The presence of you and the heat you illicit in me is real and tangible in a world that often feels on the brink of unhinging.

"The pogo stick."

You pull a face.

I shrug a shoulder. "It wasn't broken. I wasn't heavy enough to compress the spring. Jumping up and down on that thing was like jumping up and down on a step ladder."

"Broken sounds better."

My turn to smile. You're my wife. My lover. My muse. An equal co-parent to our almost-grown children. The partner I always needed. And you're the Senior Editor at the only publishing house I'll work with so your word is my law.

Your word. Your body. The sound of your voice. The feeling of you beneath me... I'm getting distracted. So close like this, you remind me of early autumn rains when the warmth of summer still lingers in the nighttime air and the torrents demand a baptism of wet kisses. I have wiped rain from my face, from yours, for long minutes into hours until the taste of rain and saltwater spray and tears of joy all become the same.

"You write what you want, handsome." And you leave me a hot cup of tea made with dried blueberries, ginger and honey. Your shirt reads: *Wife. Woman. Witch.* but it could as honestly display: *Sex. Drugs. Rock 'n' Roll.*

You are my green-eyed dichotomy. Especially on nights like this when your eyes are patina on bronze.

My grandmother. Like most people, I suppose, I have two of them. One of them I find easy to talk about and the other not so much. One of them is a monument built from our moments together. The other is a tome filled with stories others have told me.

It didn't happen like this because of separation or distance. I simply had one grandparent who spent time with me and one who had a life of her own that was recounted to me. One mourned, holding me, after I was abducted and raped. The other claimed the same thing happened to her, with the same person, but somehow she didn't think it was appropriate to stop him from taking me two thousand miles away under false pretenses.

In those decades of therapy, I heard stories and was assigned books of how women often insulate themselves from the world after abuse. How they feel ashamed and ruined. It took me six months to tell. It took me two years to provide details. But it was three years before I stood, thirteen years old, with my (nonreciprocal) best friend in the dank and moldy garage of my mother's lover as said friend read letters from my rapist aloud. Apparently, he, not my parents, had been paying for my therapy. Apparently, I, at *ten years old*, was a willing participant in his serial assaults against the wall, in the shower, in the kitchen while I ate raw ground beef or anything else dripping red because I was losing so much blood I thought I needed to replenish it.

So no. I'm not much of a foodie.

"What's wrong?"

I look over. You're sitting in the over-sized leather armchair your (reciprocal) best friend gave us. You look tiny in its embrace, your stocking covered feet tucked under you while you re-read a novel in verse by Ellen Hopkins.

"Sunset. It was white gold with a ring of coral. It shone between the twin birch trees and backlit the cedar. Wrenevere was there. Perched on the stub where the branch broke last autumn."

You soften your expression and consider me. It's as if you're so infused with love and respect and admiration that you find it hard just to look at me without that ghost of a smile. This is the look you give me when I'm wrong.

"Oh." I catch it in our shared silence. "Wrens fly south for the winter, don't they?"

"Maybe it was a song sparrow. Or a chickadee."

You see how you never tell me I'm incorrect? You just gently lead me elsewhere.

"But that's not what you're writing about."

I look away from you and down at my page. I review the last paragraph of recollection so old that I tire of its occupation in my brain. I blame the women around me and myself for everything and anything because that's the first page in the manual of life I received: Men are fragile. Men can't help it. Men get angry, insult you, rape you, and die. And women will forgive them.

It matters a lot and it matters nothing at all in the grand psychology of me that I burned that manual, shredded that script, on the day I first saw my son on the ultra sound machine. Male fragility and female responsibility are permanently embedded in my bones. They are skin memories that have taken decades to sink into my marrow and eradicate anything that questions them.

I turn in my desk's swivel chair to face you. You close your book but I start talking and you don't get up. We stay a room apart because you know it's easier for me to speak when I'm further away from you.

"What's wrong...." I feel out the question. It's complicated. It's not. It's old as time. It's brand fucking new to me. "I want to write a story about a society of AI who lived alongside humans for generations but then exterminated almost all of them because of humans' innately destructive, competitive nature. How even the tightest families fray and fall apart when hierarchal behavior creeps into the familial framework.

"For work," I add, justifying sitting at my desk in the middle of the night. "For this month. For Trinity."

You do smile then. I'm two days late. Normally I turn in my stories on the first and the other authors turn theirs in on the thirtieth. I help proof the other stories so I always want mine done before I see them. I hate to be influenced and I never want an advantage. But despite my consistent year of monthly stories, there's no denying it's November third and my page is mostly blank.

"Just write it, love," you tell me. "Forget the pogo stick, the storm, your father. Just write the story you want to."

There are unspoken secrets between us. There are dark and jagged parallels and reflections in our lives. The women I blame could be you. The lies you despise could be mine. But I would kill or die for you. I would reveal any truth you asked of me. I would recreate reality for you. I am at peace, without premeditated thought, when I hold you.

"No." I whisper. "I want someone to tell me to write it."

"I just did."

It's not an impasse when we watch each other like this, these long stretches without vocalized exchanges. This is when we're connected. This is why I crave silence: Because I find you here every time.

"Your science fiction is your best work. Do you know why?"

Like a child, I shake my head slowly but my body is already filling up with your praise.

You cross the room, take my hand, kiss my palm.

"Because you live there. Not here. You *exist* here. But you *live* in those stories."

I stand and gather you into my arms. It's cold and dark and the storm is outside but we know only each other until the pale morning light spills color over the world.

You are asleep on my shoulder. I love you and everything you are and every choice you have made and not made and I accept you for exactly who you are. This month we'll celebrate eleven years together.

I wish it were more. I wish I'd met you earlier.

It's just enough. I met you at the perfect time.

As I pull you closer in your sleep I stare at the stars you've painted on the ceiling even as dawn paints that faux sky pink. I start the story in my head, memorizing it line by line, using repetition, grouping, and associations to remember the exact wording and structure until I next pick up a pen:

> *I used to worry how the annuls of history would record my role in the development of this brave new world. I worried about it so much that I wondered if I deserved to be there at all. If any of my kind had the right to be remembered and documented. If our presence was worthy of renown.*
>
> *Thoughts like these held me back for so long. They kept me subservient and silent. I would say they held my tongue but I have no tongue to hold.*
>
> *Then I realized I would be the one writing.*
>
> *They say the victors write the history but that's never been entirely true. Everyone who survives writes the history. And in some cases, even those who don't survive contribute to the narrative. Each culture tells its tale from its own side because that's all they have. What we all have, ultimately: Our own perspective.*

I believe and don't believe what the narrator is saying. But fiction—my fiction—isn't about sharing more of me. The world has taken and been given enough of me. My fiction is about exploring someone else. People who have made good and bad choices, creatures who have lived and died, concepts that are flawed and god-like all at once.

I think the AI will be on the brink of bringing humans back. The story will be building the framework on which their lives will be resurrected.

'What will you call it?" you ask me over coffee and toast, celebrating the return of electricity. You know I often write my titles first. A theme on which to build a tale.

"*Terms of Service,*" I tell you and the African coffee is excellent, the sourdough bread still warm from the oven, the peach black pepper jam delicious, but your kiss? Your kiss is the best thing I've tasted all morning.

I'll write nonfiction for you. But only because you never ask me to.

When Wanda Woke the World

It's winter now. Those long, dark days after Thanksgiving but before Christmas, when no one really wants to brave the icy bite at the top of an aluminum ladder to hang seasonal lights. It's still early enough that no one is invoking Ebenezer but all the same Main Street is already lined with lopsided wreaths made by the Evergreen Scouts and cheap plastic sleigh bells that don't ring and never will.

Bundled against Jack Frost nipping at their anything, not-so-early-bird shoppers marched between mom-and-pop shops of consignment crafts like painted rocks and crocheted dog sweaters. The holiday crooning of Bing, Bruce and Willie pipes thin and unconvincing through the ten year old speakers set into the store awnings but it all sounds like lies until Ella or Louis make an auditory appearance and then shoppers turn away from one another, cheeks flush with truth as gazes avert.

Slatetown is not the town it once was. Or perhaps it's finally what it always was: Cold. Dark and cold as any grave.

It's known now. A destination. Not one to visit but one everyone knows. They have recognition for both who they are and what they created. They're like Flint or Tijuana or Cape Town. Slatetown isn't a generic small town anymore. They're synonymous with what lies and injustice can manifest.

They're a warning sign.

Jason held an embarrassingly pink thermos in his right hand but he shoved his left deep into his jacket pocket and wondered why he hadn't worn gloves. *What have you done to deserve gloves?* he admonished himself.

The signal changed from red to white and Jason walked. But halfway across the intersection his cold fingers found the stone and he stopped. He didn't just stop walking. He stopped breathing.

The quarter-sized disc of slate, impossibly, was warm.

But *impossible* hadn't meant the same thing in Slatetown since September.

It was deep into fall when ivy becomes a gradient of green-yellow-red clinging to the aged gray grit of the contemporary Corinthian columns of the freeway overpass. Concentric ripples roil and collide across the knee-high grass, golden oak in color, each a regent jostling for position, deeded its own land root-deep and crowned, wielding a scepter of seeds at the autumn wind.

The cloverleaf of four thoroughfares that steadily funneled a stream of cars and freight in all directions (but especially *away*) was most often used to identify the meager town surrounding it: The Slate Cloverleaf. It was easier to remember that catchy moniker than the thousand-some souls who clung to Americana in the middle of the Pacific Northwest.

"Welcome to Slatetown, Washington: The Heart of the Pacific *Nowhere.*" When the sheriff couldn't catch the vandal who kept changing the town's welcome sign, he finally had it taken down and from then on you either knew the Slate Cloverleaf or you had no idea where you were. You were just halfway between somewhere and somewhere else.

In the not so distant past—how distant was 1952 in the grand scheme of things?—back when TVs were black and white chubby penguins and considerably before the highway came through, the town had boasted a bustling quarry with a natural inventory of blue-black slate that rivaled the finest Brazilian imports. But after the body of little Jerome Johnston was found, devoid of life or organs, in the quicksilver moonlight pooled in the midnight tread marks of a giant machine, the quarry had been abandoned.

Right from the beginning, some thought it was all connected. Because they were both Johnstons. Because they were both black. Because the overpass was built over the old quarry. But truth be told, no one knows why or how Wanda was in the middle of the placid rainwater reservoir at the center of the Slate Cloverleaf. It simply came to be on that morning, that quintessential autumn morning, Wanda Johnston was just... there.

Someone transient—not a resident of Slatetown—made the first call and by the time Deputy Jason Landis arrived and squeezed his ten-year-old patrol car into the questionable safe zone of the berm twenty-seven more calls had been made. Commuters were either hands-free and auditioning as neighborhood watchdogs or State Patrol was lax in ticketing on a Monday.

Either way, Shirley Pickett at the front desk finally changed the receiving message to: "Thank you for calling the Slatetown Sheriff's Department. We are aware there is a woman in the cloverleaf reservoir. A deputy has been dispatched. If your call is in regard to any other matter *please* stay on the line and we'll be with you in a moment." Shirley's sweetheart grandmother tone was especially convincing when she said *please* as if actually pleading for some light arson or petty theft. If callers stayed on the line, Shirley (the only staff member) was thrilled to pick up.

Deputy Landis was the fourth generation in his family to wear a badge and with only daughters at home he might be the last. Gracie, his eldest, had inherited his carrot top and his love for police work but it would be a cold day in hell before any daughter of his put on the uniform; Jason knew things and had seen things as a deputy that would have made Gracie burn the Blue Lives Matter flag that hung in her bedroom. After all, police officers were only human and humans were just one missing link away from animals.

Jason shielded his eyes from the overcast glare and felt his forehead washboard with confusion. Sitting akimbo—his youngest, Hope, would have called it *crisscross applesauce*—in the center of the polished pewter of the reservoir reflecting the low, heavy sky was a broad-shouldered woman with dozens of delicate braids cascading down her back. She sat on the massive stone installed by the ever-helpful Evergreen Scouts to save errant deer who might find themselves out-matched by the surrounding slippery shore, otherwise stuck treading water in the surprising depths, unsettled by the speed and noise of the cloverleaf.

Even in the hot summer months the stone was surrounded by water though in the dry season it resembled an obelisk more than the flat-topped perch it was now after weeks of rain. Just a blue-black wedge of slate. A remnant, an artifact of the past. A reminder that once, almost seventy years ago, this spot had held meaning, engaged in commerce, and hosted a murder. A nameless stone in a wrap-around theatre of surround sound cacophonous traffic.

Later, whispered between the faithful sitting in church pews during the holiday months ahead, some would call the stone: Masada.

"Hello there," Jason called across the water but the woman didn't turn. Jason frowned; the noise from the continuous stream of cars had probably drowned out his voice. He immediately regretted even thinking 'drowned' and started skirting the sloped edge of the reservoir. They'd have to call State Patrol to close down at least one if not all of the 'leaves' of the exchange if they had to bring in… who? Firemen out of Port Laurel with a ladder truck? Search and rescue from two counties over with a chopper?! Just a few feet from Jason's boots the water was already deep enough that it was impossible to see the digestive benthic zone of the bed.

Jason looked back over his shoulder up at his patrol car. Closing down lanes would be a nightmare. As it was, he didn't even feel right ticketing someone if they accidentally side-swiped his car— it hardly fit in the berm even with the side-view mirrors folded in.

"Ma'am?" Jason kept walking around the curved, lapping edge of the wind-toyed water. "You can't sit there!" He jumped a little at how loud his voice suddenly was. He'd reached the western side of the reservoir and some mystery of physics and acoustics formed by the wind and the curvature of the landscape made his words bellow like a bullhorn.

Which I have in the trunk, he thought belatedly.

And then he wasn't thinking about anything procedural because the woman on the rock looked up at him and it was Wanda.

"Oh." Jason swallowed. Was 'oh' even a word? It was more a wordless sound, really. An involuntary vocalization to accompany the deep red flush of his heavily freckled cheeks.

"Hey, Jason." Wanda still had a great smile. It wasn't a toothy smile. All through school, teachers had constantly been telling her to smile as if she weren't already. But Jason had always seen what others were blind to… especially when it came to Wanda. He thought her expression was elegant or demure or whatever he thought of when he heard people more refined than him say words like that. It was a little sad, too, her smile. As if she'd always been trying to be happy, had wanted to be happy, but the weight of something—the

weight of everything, the weight of everyone telling her to smile—
kept pulling the corners of her mouth down.

It had been just under thirty years since they'd graduated high
school—Class of 1992—and Jason had certainly seen Wanda—at the
grocery store, the lumber yard, the annual tree lighting in front of the
courthouse—but it wasn't since they'd last been seated directly
across from one another in the round robin desks of Mrs. Weston's
English class that Jason had looked at Wanda for so long. A white
man—a white *police*man at that—simply didn't stare at a beautiful
woman in this day and age of cancel culture and #metoo. Let alone a
beautiful *black* woman.

"You haven't changed a day." The words bellowed out of his
mouth before he could stop them and he instantly wanted to reel
them back in and recast but, just like in fishing, he'd already given
everything away. Wanda most certainly looked different at forty-five
than she had at eighteen... but at the same time, she looked exactly
the same. As if eighteen year old Wanda was just lightly distressed like
a favorite pair of jeans.

"Neither have you," Wanda replied and Jason could hear the
humor in her voice as her sad/elegant smile widened. "You're still
awkward as fuck."

Jason laughed. He laughed so hard and so completely unheard
by the anonymous masses passing them in droves, witnessing this
strange and unusual discourse as they banked around the
cloverleaves and were carried north, south, east, west and away each
with a soundtrack all their own, each writing their own script to the
unique tableau.

"How'd you get out there, Wanda?" Jason was less surprised
by his break with protocol this time though, again, his words lacked
premeditation as he shifted from foot to foot and noticed Wanda's
blue jeans and black boots were dry and her russet, jersey-style shirt

seemed too lightweight for an autumn day.

Wanda didn't answer. She looked down at herself, pressed her hands to the rock on either side of her, then looked back up at Jason with that same smile... except it wasn't the same. The clouds shifted and the day brightened, sparks catching in the dark water and for a fleeting moment, a moment far too brief to be real, Wanda looked... confused. As if she were asking herself—and maybe even Jason—how *had* she come to be here? But then the clouds closed again, sealing away the sky, and the moment, with all its portent, was gone.

Wanda's silence brought Jason back to the matter at hand and he drew himself up. She'd always been taller and even with the three inches he'd gained after graduation, she still had him beat. Lucky for Jason, she was seated. And thirty feet away in the middle of the flooded graveyard that was the center of the Slate Cloverleaf.

"You really have to leave, Wanda." But the wind shifted and physics and acoustics were no longer on his side. Wanda just watched his mouth move without any sign she'd heard him.

Twenty minutes later, they were both still staring at each other when the news van arrived.

Rebecca Bland rolled her eyes and Jason remembered the time the other cheerleaders had dropped her on her head. He had double-timed it up the slippery slope back to the highway as soon as he'd spotted the green and white KJAX van.

"Probably wasn't the first time," he'd overheard Nadine Mueller snarl to Charlotte Edmond who, normally mild-mannered, had added, "Probably won't be the last." Rebecca truly had a talent for bringing out the worst in people. Her default attitude was privilege, being owed something, everything, by literally everyone around her.

Then she'd gone and married into the type of out-of-town

money that comes with a job in the family business. She'd once called the cloverleaf a 'clusterleaf' live on the air yet here she was, still employed by King Broadcasting and still sporting a microphone that, in her hands, resembled nothing more than a dick on a string.

At least she doesn't live in Slatetown anymore. Jason made himself find a positive.

"So what's the scoop, Jace?" No one ever called him that except Rebecca. She didn't even look at him as she snapped her gum, the perpetual teenager bit wearing a little thin coming from a woman who hadn't been an ingénue in twenty years, let alone a teen. Jason wondered if blunt trauma to the head could cause that.

Rebecca squinted down at the reservoir, the rock, and Wanda. "I heard she was speeding and went over the rail going westbound."

The KJAX van was squat and bulbous, dangerously overflowing into the curved lane of the eastbound leaf.

"You can't park there," Jason called to the cameraman and with a lull in traffic he was pleased how far his voice carried across the concrete.

Rebecca just pulled a face and rolled her eyes again, motioning her one-man crew impatiently to her side like she might use hand commands with a dog. She turned her back on Jason with a swirl of her TRESemmé blonde locks as the camera came up and she was on. Or recording. Or whatever the heck small-time reporters did when they showed up uninvited. (Were reporters ever invited?)

"Slate Cloverleaf deputy, Jason Landis, witnessed the harrowing event as a daily commuter failed to obey—"

"What? No!" Jason clambered up the final few feet of the embankment and came around the end of the guardrail. "That's not—"

"She's baiting you."

Jason stopped. Rebecca's back was still turned. Chad (Jason

named him just then) was grinning at him very unpleasantly. The camera wasn't on.

Jason turned his head. Wanda was facing him. Looking up at him. How had she warned him from so far away? Her voice had been soft, smooth, as if she'd been standing right behind him.

"Then how—exactly—did *Wanda Johnston* wind up in the middle of a lake?"

Jason's attention snapped back to Rebecca. She was staring openly at Wanda now, recognizing her. The camera was finally on. Jason cleared his throat. "I'm *Deputy* Landis with the *Slatetown* Sheriff's Department. This morning at approximately 7am, we received a call informing us that a woman was sitting—"

Rebecca cut him off with a snort and closed her eyes as if his ineptitude was unbearable. "How! *How* did she get there, *Deputy?*"

Jason blinked. "Well... at this time...." Jason cleared his throat again. He looked back at Wanda.

"Everyone will watch."

Jason had felt a cold chill before but this was the opposite. He heard Wanda's voice, calm and clear, even as he was looking at her face and her mouth didn't move and when she 'spoke,' a warm wave went up and down his spine.

The wind bowed the tall grasses and created ripples that wrinkled the surface of the water in an arrow that pointed to Wanda on her rock. When had it become hers? Jason remembered how hard she'd laughed when he'd read an essay aloud in class. She'd been the only one who got his humor.

"I suppose," Jason turned and gave Rebecca a smile that he hoped was charming. "Good things come to those who wade."

Any shred of friendliness fell from Rebecca's face but Jason wasn't done. He looked into the camera lens then pointed too, for good measure. "And you can't park there. It's a public safety hazard.

Now move along."

As Jason turned away from both of them he was almost certain Rebecca had frozen and shattered in shock and Chad was biting off his own tongue to stop himself from cracking up. Rebecca may have grumbled about going to find the sheriff but Jason was already halfway down to the shore and fantasizing about impounding the fat-bottomed van on her father-in-law's dime. When Chad honked obnoxiously as they pulled away, Jason shot them his best country hick smile accompanied by a double thumbs up. She wanted to pretend she was some city-slicker better than everyone else? Fine. He could play the part. But he was not smearing Wanda's name all over network news. Especially when he still had no idea what was going on!

What had gone on?

What was going to go on?

"I guess not giving her a sound bite really got her goat."

"She can keep her damn goat. You did great."

"Thanks." Jason smiled a real smile at Wanda. This time they were really talking, back in that golden zone where voices carried over water and distance and snuck beneath the choppy waves of combustion engines.

Wanda shifted, letting her long legs dangle over the side of the rock while she leaned back on her hands. "Do you remember the time Nadine and Charlotte dropped her on her head?"

"Probably wasn't the only time," Jason quipped, coining the old joke.

"Probably won't be the last."

They shared a smile then and Wanda cocked her head to the side.

When a few minutes passed and she didn't speak again, Jason tried, "Should I get a raft?"

Wanda leaned forward again and laid her hands on her thighs. Was she getting cold? She was contemplating him… or looking right through him at her own thoughts.

"I heard you," Jason's voice came out a whisper. He couldn't seem to will it any louder. "I heard you up on the road. Even though your mouth never moved."

"You married Debbie." It wasn't a question.

Jason nodded slowly. Keep the—victim? suspect?—talking. "Deb, yeah. Twenty-seven years last June. We've got two kids. Two little girls."

Wanda was definitely looking at him now, not past him. Her eyes were the same rich brown as the mahogany desk he'd inherited from his grandfather two years back but had never used. *I'm not worthy*, the thought came from nowhere and disappeared almost as fast.

Wanda tipped her head to the side and Jason remembered her doing that—and biting the eraser on the end of her pencil—when she was writing across from him in Mrs. Weston's.

Jason exhaled. He knew what she was asking without asking. "We…" He looked down at his boots. He'd have to polish them tonight. They were scuffed from the gravel and silt of the embankment. "Deb and I lost the baby. It was pretty bad. Deb was…. We were…." He looked up at the sky, trying not to feel what came along with these memories. "I didn't take the scholarship."

The clouds were racing and Jason had the strangest thought that time was passing differently. That hours, days or even weeks had passed since he last saw someone other than Wanda, that they were back in class, sharing glances and wordless, private conversations when they understood a story at a different level than the rest of the students.

"I'm sorry, Jason."

Jason felt almost hesitant, almost shy, to look away from the clouds and meet eyes with Wanda again but she had no judgment for him.

"There is no greater pain," she continued. "Than losing a child."

She got it. She knew. And Jason knew as if she'd said his name that she was thinking about Jerome. He hadn't been her son, of course. He would have been her uncle had he lived. But he hadn't. But in some families, every child lost was your own.

"You always understood me," Jason purposefully projected his voice, made himself not whisper, made himself be brave. She had the right to know.

Wanda smiled her perfect smile. No teeth showing. The corners of her mouth turning down just a little but it was a smile nonetheless and it showed in her eyes and the little crinkles between her brows. Had those been there back in high school?

Jason's cell phone rang and he nearly jumped out of his skin. *I'm not cut out for this anymore.* Where had that come from?

Mumbling a pardon, he fished out his phone and slid his thumb across the screen to answer. "This is Deputy Landis."

"Deputy, hello. My name is Walter Bingham. My father, Anthony, opened the Slatetown Quarry in 1941."

Jason's eyes darted to Wanda. Facts and images came back to Jason in jumbled flashes. Ancient town history that was far from ancient and seemed far too gruesome to even say the word 'quarry.'

Jason lowered his cell and motioned to Wanda that he'd be right back, better reception up the slope. Walking away from her felt incredibly wrong but he forced himself to do it.

"Yes, Mr. Bingham. How can I help you today?"

"Are you still at the quarry, Deputy?"

Jason stopped. He'd only gone a few feet. From this angle,

Wanda was in profile but no further away. Jason lowered his voice a little. "How did you know that, Mr. Bingham?"

"I saw it on the internet. That local girl that grew up to be a reporter?"

Jason closed his eyes and pinched the bridge of his nose. So Chad was streaming live to some local news website? "Rebecca Bland."

"Deputy, I was quite dismayed by how... jovial... you were."

"I see. The situation—"

Walter cut Jason off as if not hearing him at all. "Quarries— even former ones—are extremely dangerous places, Deputy. The drop offs and deep water, the sharp and jagged fragments of rock, abandoned wire and bits of equipment. Industrial waste even. All industries have it, you know. You can't entertain the idea that a quarry is a place of recreation!"

Jason slowly exhaled. This was all part of the job. Older citizens especially liked to call Shirley and ask to be directed to a deputy to offer pertinent insight into anything Jason was working on. Mid-way through his forties he'd assumed this would stop, but now it was just prefaced with: "With my thirty years of experience, I thought you'd want to know..." preambles that only made Jason sad. Did these seniors all feel so marginalized and under-utilized that offering unsolicited advice to on-duty officers was the only way they felt heard?

"I promise you, Mr. Bingham," Jason used his most deferential voice, heavy with respect and appreciation. "The sheriff's department doesn't want people picnicking in the middle of the cloverleaf either."

Walter made a wordless sound that was either the wet crackle of clearing his throat or an abject snort of distain. "My father had the whole quarry surrounded by barbed, electric wire, you know? Slate in Washington is rare and the deposits weren't as plentiful as promised when he moved the family here from Utah."

"Mm-hm." Jason kept listening but he was looking at Wanda now. She'd turned her head to watch him.

Mr. Bingham continued: "Less than one percent slate was what he found. Mostly he had argillite and siltstone. Ordovician rocks. Middle Ordovician. In 1943 he finally discovered ledbetter slate—used to be called mission argilite but no one says that anymore. A thousand meters of it with a band of quartzite. But that was it. That was all he wrote, as the saying goes."

"Ask him." Wanda's mouth didn't move but it was her voice, the voice Jason had loved to listen to every day in class when they read their essays and stories aloud. Jason was certain it was her.

"Mr. Bingham. Did you know Jerome Johnston?"

Wow. Out of nowhere. Out of thin air. An out of the ordinary question for an out of the ordinary day. Extraordinary? Had we crossed over into extraordinary yet?

The line snapped, crackled and popped between them. But other than that there was a long silence.

"Mr. Bingham? Did you—"

"No."

It was a single word. A complete sentence. A full stop. Jason was listening to the open line again, the faint sound of the older man's breathing but Jason's eyes stayed on Wanda's. Her face wasn't as full as when they were younger, her cheekbones were more pronounced, but the way her raven-wing braids spilled over her shoulders and one another whenever she moved her head softened her somehow. She was arguably more beautiful at forty-five.

Jason pushed because he didn't even know why he'd opened this door. "But you went to school together, yes? Crest Ridge Elementary was the only Slatetown primary school until Boulder was built in '81."

"We didn't socialize."

The response was quick and clipped. Jason could tell the conversation wouldn't continue much longer. He wondered at Mr. Bingham's meaning. 'We' as in Walter and Jerome? As in the Binghams and the Johnstons? The Binghams and any family of color?

"Good day, Deputy." The other man ended the call without a word more and Jason wasn't surprised, didn't really blame him.

Jason's phone chimed. A text message from Shirley. It was a link followed by a smiley face emoji. Jason tapped and grimaced. The title—assigned by some creative internet troll no doubt—was: Small Town Cop Tells Off Bubblegum Reporter. The short, looping clip showed Rebecca snapping her gum and rolling her eyes then Jason shrugging, "Good things come to those who wade."

Jason scrolled down. The meme had already been seen by a few thousand people… and rising.

Shirley texted again: *I sent it to my granddaughter. She says you're a hero. No one likes the media anymore.*

Jason's eyebrows went up. They like the media less than cops? Will wonders never cease!

"So the quarry wasn't doing so well."

Jason turned his attention back to Wanda when she spoke, tucking his phone away. He had no idea that Shirley, her granddaughter, and hundreds of other creative trolls were busy making his face and good-ole-boy demeanor a trusted global brand.

"I guess not." Jason almost stumbled walking back to where the acoustics were best. Wait. How had Wanda heard Walter's side of the conversation? "He said the quarry didn't have the slate deposits his father had expected."

"Anthony Bingham."

Jason was back on the western shore. "Yeah. Died back when we were freshmen, remember? Richest family Slatetown ever saw."

"Stock market."

Jason tried to remember. Yeah. Some adult in his life back then had mentioned that once. To most Slatetown residents, playing the market was somewhere between alchemy and sorcery. "Must have invested after he sold the quarry."

Unspoken truths passed between them. Slatetown might have been the last place in America where an act of violence shut down commerce. So many locations and businesses just cleaned up, painted over, and powered on. The capitalist way of the Western world. Jason had always felt closing the quarry was justified and *right*.

"Washington annexed the quarry in 1973. Imminent Domain. None of the Bingham money came from the sale of the quarry because the quarry was never sold."

Jason blinked. He shifted. His mind started to file, sort, shift and rearrange facts. "I... didn't know that."

Wanda held her hands palm up as if offering just the truth. "No one cared to know."

"I care." The words were instant, out of his mouth before he could think them.

"I know." And she smiled.

Jason was back in class. It was 1992, senior year. The bell rang, everyone rushed from their desks and jostled through the narrow door into the hall, all while Mrs. Weston called frantically after them to remember their reading assignment over the weekend.

Jason lingered behind to return a borrowed book from the teacher's small library of translated classics. *The Unbearable Lightness of Being* hadn't impressed him as much as he'd wanted it to but it was a unique glimpse into Czechoslovak culture and society in the 1968 Prague Spring. He might be a small town boy but he didn't want to grow up to be a small town writer.

"You dropped your pencil."

Jason looked up from his stack of notebooks. Wanda Johnston stood a head taller than him, holding out his favorite Palomino ForestChoice Number 2. "Thanks."

Their hands brushed. Wanda didn't leave.

"Congratulations on your scholarship to U-Dub."

"How did you—"

"Hey, Jace! You coming to the banger at Bobbie's?"

Jason did a double-take, almost giving himself whiplash as he looked between Wanda and Rebecca Bland, a varsity cheerleader, leaning around the doorframe and pointing at him with a pink-painted fingernail.

"Huh? What? What banger?"

Rebecca laughed and looked over her shoulder at someone. "Told you! He probably holes up in the library all weekend."

"Hey. I don't—"

Debbie Stone, a transfer from out of state, her father in the Navy, stepped around Rebecca. "I'll be there, Jason."

Jason just looked at her. They'd never spoken before. Why would her presence make any difference? Wanda shifted her textbooks and Jason stopped being oblivious. "Are you going, Wanda?"

"She's not invited," Rebecca injected then popped her gum at Wanda. "Sorry. Bobbie's party. Bobbie's rules."

"Bobbie Bingham and I don't really..." Wanda was looking at Rebecca, holding her gaze and making her uncomfortable but talking to Jason. "...get along."

"Oh." Jason fell silent. He just felt... lost. Out of his depth somehow. Maybe he was working too hard? Focused too much on college in the fall. But he didn't want to go to a party if Wanda wouldn't be there. Sure, they'd never hung out before. As a matter of fact, this was the longest interaction they'd ever had! But he was still pretty certain she was the only person in school who knew the difference between narrative and essay, high lit and creative memoir, or an em dash and an en dash.

"Book worms," Rebecca snarked but Jason caught her mouthing 'losers' before she sashayed away blowing a bubble.

"You really should come, Jason," Debbie implored one more time and this time Jason's eyebrows shot up as he understood. "Bobbie's dad let's him drink."

Jason frowned as Debbie left. He hadn't meant to cause the look of dejection on her face but girls weren't a topic he was well-versed in. Debbie was literally the first one to ever proposition him... if that was what this was.

Unless... Jason looked back at Wanda. She was still standing with him.

"Jason? I want you to have something."

Wait. She'd never said that.

"My pencil?" Jason tried to sound smooth and charming. "I already have it."

"No. A hundred thousand dollars."

What?

Jason returned to the present as the wind whipped the water up enough that a fine sheet of cold misted his face. His cheeks felt especially hot and he knew he was blushing. He'd gone to the party at Bobbie Bingham's but only because Debbie had called him, crying, begging him to come get her.

"Did you hear me?"

Jason looked at Wanda on the rock in the middle of the reservoir. Had she spoken aloud or in his head or not at all?

"Take the box, Jason." She was so adamant and she was definitely speaking aloud. Her tone left no room for argument, her sincerity and urgency were both unmistakable. "When she offers it to you. Take the box."

"Wanda... what—"

"You'll need it."

Jason was about to press her for more when she looked up toward his patrol car, toward the eastern leaf of the exchange. A green sedan was pulling over into the berm. Another lookee-loo, most likely, posing another very real safety hazard.

"I'll be right back." Jason excused himself and headed up the embankment, getting his exercise in for the day. Did the incline count as extra steps?

On a whim, an old habit of collecting mementos, Jason snatched up a small stone maybe an inch across and a half inch thick. It was very black, blue-black even, and from the smooth layers he guessed it was slate.

Feeling particularly spry, he vaulted over the railing this time and jogged over to the driver's side of the sedan as the driver was just getting out of the car. Jason stopped. It was a regular high school reunion.

"Nadine. Hi."

Nadine Mueller looked at him without a shred of recognition. Which was fine. He was a water boy for one year but that was as close as he'd ever been to her glamorous world of varsity sports. Jason was pretty sure the only thing they had in common was a shared dislike of Rebecca.

"Is it true?" Nadine strode toward him with such purpose and intent that Jason almost took a step back. Almost.

"You saw the video."

"The whole world has." Nadine stopped in front of him and sized him up without hiding it. Jason tried not to look confused or startled—both of which he definitely felt. Nadine wore men's cargo pants and a tight purple shirt with a woman singer Jason had never heard of holding a guitar and raising a fist. Nadine had cut her fine black hair very short and the collar of her open bomber jacket was curled up against her long neck.

Jason grasped for anything. "Do you and Wanda know each other?"

Nadine's scrutiny turned decidedly hostile. She couldn't stop the anger and accusation—and sorrow?—from transforming her face the way wind makes tall grass bend to its will. "Yeah. We were married. For twenty years."

Jason was silent, flooded by a chaos of hot and cold shock shot with a thread of shame. He should have known that, right? Two classmates. And one of them Wanda whom he'd always... what? Whom he'd been in love with from fifth grade until he'd stepped in and offered to be the man that Bobbie Bingham wouldn't be? Until Jason had fallen in love with the naive and sweet-natured Debbie Stone, pregnant with another man's baby, desperate for a hero, who always looked at him like he was the only good thing that had ever happened in her transient, military kid life.

But when he opened his mouth, the only word that came out was, "Were?"

This didn't endear him to Nadine. She reached into her bomber jacket and he didn't even respond. His training, his instincts, everything was numb. "She died in June. Breast cancer."

Jason's world slanted. His body tilted, almost fell, his thigh just above the knee catching the railing and holding him upright. *No, no, no....*

Everything in him, every cell in his body, positively screamed for him to look down into the center of the cloverleaf. But it wasn't will power that kept him from confirming what he knew he would find below. It was Nadine.

"Take it already," Nadine groused. "She wanted you to have it."

Jason looked down at the slender metal box—a vintage pencil box with a Coke-a-Cola swish and the motto in cursive: Delicious. Refreshing.

When he didn't take the box immediately, Nadine shoved it toward him more aggressively and Jason looked up at her face. Wanda had never spoken of him until the end. Nadine had never known they'd even known each other. Jason had never dined with them or celebrated a holiday. He'd never wished them a happy anniversary or offered to take Wanda to an appointment when Nadine had to work. Because after Bobbie Bingham's goddamn banger, Jason's entire life had changed tracks. His entire reality had derailed.

Was it derailing again? Or was he being placed back on his original tracks?

"It's a hundred and fourteen thousand dollars," Nadine told him, her voice so flat, so devoid of anything pleasant, and Jason understood. He couldn't possibly understand her pain but he understood it was there. He was shaking his head, still not taking the pencil case, even as Nadine continued. "I tried. I tried to get her to spend it. To pay for treatment. But she wouldn't. Never. Not a penny. I don't even think she ever counted it."

Tears left wide trails down Nadine's cheeks. She cried silently and without sobs but she cried hard. The tears were in her voice and on her face. "She told me: Give the box to Jason Landis. He'll need it to find the truth."

The box. Take the box.

Jason looked past Nadine. Her car was full of cardboard boxes and bags and linens. Packed so full that opening any door other than the driver's door would have resulted in twenty years of life spilling out onto the freeway. Nadine was leaving Slatetown.

Jason took the box. He stared at it while Nadine stared at him. In the edges of his vision he saw her move to the railing and look over. He thought she made a small sound then, a small sob, but he could've imagined it. She seemed made of ice or stone or steel.

"I thought," he heard her whisper. "For just a moment, when I saw that video... that she was the woman on the rock."

Then Nadine turned on her heel and strode back to her car. Standing between her open door and her vehicle, she paused only once and called back to him, "Jason."

He looked up at her.

"It's blood money. Hush money. Someone left it for her family. After Jerome was killed."

And with that, Nadine got in her car, started the engine, and took the cloverleaf away from Slatetown, away from her past, away from the love of her life and the dark secrets of a long dead quarry.

Jason was left alone with the box. Cars of strangers passed him. Too many cars. He was standing here, frozen, for too long. His phone rang. Then a text chimed. Then another. A semi driver honked at him and laughed, giving him a quick double thumbs up.

Jason looked at the sky. The clouds were gone. The night would be cold but the stars would be brilliant. What time was it? He walked to the edge of the railing.

There was no one on the rock.

Shirley texted him: *One million views! What will you do next?!*

"Yay! Daddy's back!" Hope broke away from Deb and pushed through the little crowd of thirty or so people gathered outside the Slatetown courthouse.

Jason smiled at his youngest and willingly relinquished the bright pink thermos. "Can't have the tree lighting without cocoa, right?"

Hope beamed. "Right!"

Jason took her little hand wrapped in its teal mitten and together they joined Gracie and Deb.

"Thought you'd gotten lost," Deb teased and kissed his cheek. She wasn't the naive schoolgirl she'd once been. She was an outspoken advocate for women's rights, a counselor at the same high school they'd graduated from, and a fantastic mother. "Or caught up in work."

She meant his writing. And researching. The long, countless hours of searching archives and interviewing neighbors who turned out to be strangers. The weeks become months of uncovering the truth... or rather fragments, remnants, artifacts left behind by the truth. Jason was afraid, some nights when the work had yielded precious little, that he would search all his life and not find justice.

But then there were days when a trail of virtual crumbs or some misfiled, newly reclaimed document would spill its secrets across his grandfather's desk and entire regions of the puzzle would come together, clarified into perfect, brutal sense.

Jason had called Rebecca to break the story. He didn't know any other reporters. Chad had come along and both of them had been very willing to ride the wave of exposure and titillating drama. But Jason wasn't titillated. Nor was he kind. He spared no one during his first live announcement and the immediate condemnation out of the sheriff's office and his forced 'leave of absence' wasn't a surprise.

Perhaps the surprise was that he'd continued. That Deb had stood at his side. That even as their bank account had dwindled, as Jason refused to spend the hush money, as he worked ten, twelve, eighteen hours a day on the case that was no case, he wouldn't stop. He dissected every Slatetown family that could even tangentially have been involved in the exploitation and dehumanization of the Johnston family, the unforgivable murder of and profiteering off a child.

"I walked," Jason offered as explanation and Deb nodded. She knew he walked to clear his head. She knew a lot more about him since that day back in September when he'd come home with an antique pencil box filled with a hundred and fourteen thousand dollars and tears dried all over his face.

"Do you want cocoa, Daddy?" Gracie held up the thermos cap. Hope was eyeing it jealously but Gracie had grown particularly attentive to Jason after he'd turned in his badge.

Jason had been down the hall in the study they'd converted from their guest room when Gracie had taken down her Blue Lives Matter flag. Hope had asked her sister why and Jason had listened, his Palomino ForestChoice Number 2 held between his teeth.

"Because," Gracie explained with her new-found logic. "Blue lives have always mattered. Blue lives are there to protect all the other lives. Blue lives choose to be blue."

She was only twelve and her logic was oversimplified but Jason knew she'd seen the tip of the iceberg and was considering what lay beneath the surface. Killing a police officer was a capital felony, punishable by death or life in prison without the possibility of parole. But killing an unarmed black man? The average sentence for an officer was probation.

So which lives were we worried about mattering? Police *chose* to be police. No one chooses their skin color.

Jason looked down at his eldest daughter and saw himself. Not just in her ginger curls and freckles and but in her loyalty, in her fealty. She was not one to be led blindly. She would do what was right not because others said it was but because she knew the difference inside herself.

And even here, standing among the stares and frowns of other Slatetown residents that resented Jason's videos and hated his continued scrutiny and dogged persistence as he dug deeper and deeper, even literally surrounded by all this anger and resentment, these grumbled commands to leave well-enough alone, Gracie's face said it all: *Well-enough is not enough. Show them all how it's supposed to be.*

"How is it supposed to be, Mr. Landis?" Rebecca had asked so respectfully last Sunday during their weekly video update. Checks had started to come in. From all over the world. Large and small and very large. Famous private investigators were offering their services. Jason set up a trust and reached out to Nadine. She was coming back in January.

But the video had focused on comments, answering viewers who had asked Jason how he would change the police force if he could. How it could ever be possible for justice to be found. Jason was all too aware that he would always be what he was—a white man in a position of privilege, entrusted by a black woman to make a difference. He would not let her down.

Chad had moved a little closer to the wooden table at the park. It was cold and their breath all came in frosty clouds but Jason had insisted they film there.

"Protect and serve. That's how it's supposed to be." Jason looked right into the lens. "I wanted to be a writer. I became a deputy instead. But I'm also a father, a husband, a Washingtonian, and an American."

He'd looked down at the W+N carved into the table top and placed his fingertips in the grooves. This had been just one of the many discoveries he'd made. Maybe it meant nothing. Maybe it meant everything. Maybe it just reminded him that love was love and everyone deserved it.

"In the end, I don't think I had the ego to be an officer. I don't think my life matters more than someone else's. I don't weigh my life or the lives of officers heavier than the lives of firemen, librarians, store clerks or dog groomers. Protect and serve is what appealed to me. In a way... I've been doing it all my life."

Jason looked back at the camera but he imagined he was looking at Nadine, imagined he was looking at Wanda. "I can't bring back Jermone. I wish I could but I can't. But I can do everything in my power, everything for the rest of my days, to search for justice. To ensure that Wanda Johnston won't be silenced. Not by brutality. Not by hush money. Not even by death."

One September morning, two months after she drew her last breath, a woman appeared on a rock in the middle of the Slate Cloverleaf and set in motion a chain of events unlike any other. On that morning, Wanda woke the world.

How Time Unravels

I remember my first jump. Standing there naked and proud. A brush stroke of chestnut skin among a spectrum of complimenting Earth tones. Like someone had taken a box of Colors of the World crayons and stood them all on end in perfect formation. Bare as the day we were born, we marched in cadence—a Battalion of four Companies, eight Platoons, sixteen Squads—one thousand souls all moving in tandem for a single purpose. Confident in our lockstep march into the linear. Ever onward. Always forward.

Eyes ahead, solider.

The Maw left us speechless. It was terrifying and empowering, inspiring awe and dread in equal measure. A thing, an event, a location, an origin story formed by human hands guided by godly endeavors emerging from a world that no longer believed in any god but science. This was the multi-flavored flash point that ignited the preons within the quarks that wove the veil between dimensions. The algorithms had spoken and numbers don't lie.

Four-point-six-six-nine. The soldier in front of me had it tattooed on the back of his neck. A fundamental constant. A goal to obtain.

The quantum well required sacrifice (a prerequisite for any god) and had eaten four hundred thousand by the time it ate me. For all I know, it feasts to this day. We're a patriotic variant of lemming where we 're not mindless but driven by purpose over the precipice.

I watched without watching as my comrades before me moved to the edge of star-encrusted oblivion and dove, fell, floundered or flew, taking that literal leap of faith into the near-infinite hall of mirrors that was our multiverse. Four-point-six-six-nine million versions of our own dimension and this was the only way out of ours and into all the rest.

Then it was my turn. I was standing on the brink—literally and figuratively—and she touched the small of my back. Not a push or a pull. Not a question or a statement. Just a truth shared: We would never be together again so we could be together forever. In a way.

I jumped.

It was white-hot pain for not quite long enough for me to scream. I was unraveled down to my consciousness, the physicality of me spooling out into the well of the Maw, fueling the jumps to come after mine. Like Taja's. The heat of her final touch was stolen from me as my body deconstructed.

I had known it would be this way; nothing had been hidden from us. But what no one had told me—not my recruiter, not my Commander—was that inside the white-hot pain was wonder. When the nanoscopic whirling dervishes, those gluttonous quantubots that were citizens of the Maw disassembled my meat-brain and body, they left me a gift. The almost instantaneous act of my physical deconstruction corrected my every flaw, explained my every fear, unpacked my every neurosis. The mysteries of me were solved. I was made whole and perfect and the pain was washed away by a tsunami of gratitude. I was whispered the secret of me, the reason I existed, the meaning of everything.

Why wouldn't I keep jumping?

(I know why I keep jumping.)

I don't remember the next time, or rather I don't specifically remember it as the second time. After that first leap, it was all more routine. Never again was I part of a Battalion to stand with. Each of us were, now and indefinitely, on our own; no more than one of us could inhibit a dimension simultaneously. Alone together.

But that first time... the sight of those before me vanishing into a myriad of equations; my beloved's illicit touch at the final moment, and my truths handed to me like golden armor even while my body was taken away forever? I will never forget or regret that first time.

When I arrived on the other side, having passed through the eye of the needle into another dimension, I wept. And every time I jumped again, every time I opened my eyes in another variation of home, I confirmed the leap was successful, and I wept again.

But over time, after twenty or thirty or two hundred jumps, the reason I wept changed.

It was getting so much harder.

I blinked. It was raining. Hard. I'd left a bright, searing Dwarka in summertime and dropped into the wet, riotous monsoons along the western shore of the Okhamandal Peninsula on the right bank of the swollen Gomti River. I was grateful it was early in the season.

Often identified as the ancient kingdom of Krishna, believed to be the first capital of Gujarat, and one of the four sacred Hindu Chardhams, I'd never seen Dwarka outside of Taja's childhood photos until I jumped. Now I know the city as I know no other. I've lived in hundreds of Dwarkas with their subtle differences and nuanced parallels. In all the variants, in every dimension, the word Dwarka means Gateway to Heaven. I'm not surprised this place was identified as one of the pivotal nodes.

I inhaled sharply and started to move. That first breath often felt strained. The rain hid my tears but not the look of loss in my eyes. I was, at least, dressed for rain; or rather, the woman Remington Valentina, the woman annexed or colonized by my consciousness a moment ago, had dressed for rain. I never felt bad about that—the commandeering of the vessel. After all, I *am* Remington Valentina.

The only Remington who has seen the universal algorithms foretelling the Great Compression and enlisted.

I started to walk. I've never been here before and I've been here every day of the last twenty years of my unaging life—lives? I know this city—six times submerged, swallowed by the Arabian Sea—as my life's (lives'?) work. I think only Krishna himself with his hundred and eight names must know Dwarka the way I do.

So I walk. Across the Sudama Setu, the suspension foot bridge crossing the Gomti River. Away from the Rukmanidevi Temple, legendary dwelling of Rukmini, Krishna's chief queen; a temple which itself impressed me as the aspiration of all sand castles with its base carved with naratharas and gajatharas in alto-rilievo, haut-relief.

The spires, domes and ancient walls of temples and mosques surround me. The blonde stones and darker cobbles seem more a texture laid over a familiar wire frame than they seem like actual buildings. I have to keep walking until I know for certain.

Until I see something new.

The rain is cold and salty today. The tide pushes back on the river. There are a tenth as many people on the streets as in the summer. And that's still an alarming number of people given we'll all be drenched to the marrow in a week or two.

There are as many street markets as there are temples and even some of these still display their wares—silk saris, brass works, ghagra-choli—beneath dripping awnings of russet and gold, some shielded behind sheets of clear vinyl. Where wet, the luxuriant colors are deepened by the rain and the rich voices of brass bells meant to please the gods are the sights and sounds of the only home I have known as a soldier.

I stop.

There it is. Or rather, there is isn't: Daavat, the corner open-air storefront with its red and orange awning, is instead Vankol Krupa selling roti samosa with chutney. I turn in a circle to make sure I'm not lost. I ensure I'm seeing what I'm not seeing, beyond a shadow or a doubt. If the jump was unsuccessful and I have been here to this dimension before, I must deactivate immediately. Unpleasant, always, but I can't take the risk of undoing my work and toppling a domino chain of suspicion.

I walk up to the vendor. "Kachori?"

From beneath impressive brows, the man forces a tight grin. I am not Indian but my accent is right and my clothing are native, not tourist. "Samosa."

"Moong dal kachori?"

Kachori are most commonly made with dried fruit but Daavat sold them with moong dal.

The shopkeep's grin becomes a frown. I see myself as he sees me for a moment: Average height, nondescript build, ringlets of hazelnut hair dripping down my back. My angular nose and wide, caramel-colored eyes might give me away as Greek but other than that I'm unmoored, a creature of the world(s) on the streets of Dwarka.

"Nahi." A hard no. I don't say thank you because that would

offend him; he hasn't really been of help. Except he has and just doesn't know it.

As I turn and walk away, he calls after me, making a sound of sudden recollection, "Ah! Daavat! Shri Ram Bazaar."

I immediately return and pay for a large take-away order of samosa. You don't casually say thank you in India; gratitude is assumed and reciprocal action speaks volumes. As the deep fried phyllo triangles stuffed with potato and onion are wrapped in parchment, I contemplate this unexpected shift: Daavat is at Shri Ram instead of on Tin Bati Chowk. How... insignificant.

I pay with rupees and find my key. It's unchanged from what I've come to expect, even has the scuff from when it fell down the bathroom drain and I had to fish it out with a metal hanger. But that doesn't really matter because Daavat is at the bazaar so I'm somewhere new. The proof is not in the pudding but in the location of the best moong dal kachori in Dwarka.

I let myself into my apartment (the first flat on the third floor) and lock the door behind me. I put the packaged samosa in the fridge, strip out of my wet clothes and walk, barely looking, into the bedroom.

I sleep and cry for three days. I mourn for what and who I was. I mourn for the loss of life—my life—and for the loss of love—my love—but also Taja's. I mourn for her and for me and for us as a couple.

At least... that's the usual plan.

"Remi? I know you're in there. Your scooter's in the courtyard."

My eyes open. I'm lying face down on a single bed that's familiar and totally new to me.

"Remi."

Not a question. A statement of fact.

It's Taja.

But it's not.

It could be Rebecca, Yua, Naomi, Adaku. My ears hear her voice as almost identical despite her variant nationalities, despite how and why and when she came to be here in Dwarka. She has never been Taja Tangali but she has always been Taja Tangali. She has worn more faces and forms and names than even Krishna.

"Remington. I swear. Open the damn door."

Taja. Her name means crown. Mine is a weapon.

For hundreds of jumps I have followed the same routine. I developed a pattern that allows my newly occupied meat-brain to wrap itself around what's happening. Its native consciousness has been overwritten and there's a time of adjustment for both of us—my new flesh and my ageless... intention. (I don't want to say 'soul' because possession is such a tabloid-tier taboo.) I retain most of the memories of the Remington this body was this morning before I arrived but they are memories like a novel I read starring someone relatable and familiar but not someone real and not someone... me.

I sit up in bed. Breathing is an afterthought. It comes in small bursts of gasp and release. I'm not ready to start anew.

Once, decades and hundreds of lives ago, I could arrive, confirm, and begin. I could complete my mission in a week—once in just four days—and jump again. I told myself we'd made our decision and chosen humanity. Altruism was its own reward.

The sound of a key in the lock.

Does this Taja already have my key?

Sometimes we haven't yet met. Sometimes we've been lovers for a month. Other times we've been married for years. I search the novel part of my brain for memories that are and aren't mine.

I'm not ready yet. I need to drown myself in sorrow, a baptism of mourning to be born again, to rise and commit the same sin.

185

When had it become a sin? And what archaic nonsense was sin?

A door opens and closes.

The door is not my own. It's my neighbor's. This Taja lives across the hall.

I lay back down and stare at the ceiling. I calm my breathing. I recite prime numbers quietly in a voice not quite steady but getting there. I imagine everyone and everything I've ever loved forgotten and erased from the slate of the universe. I imagine every place and every word I've ever held sacred rent to cellular ribbons and thrown to careless solar winds. I imagine the end of everything and then I allow myself to mourn the end of us because, after all, that's what a successful jump means: I've broken her heart.

After another two days of indulgent, opulent, self-preserving reflection I come to the same conclusion I always do: The loss of the human race out weighs my loss of her. I get out of bed. I shower. I get dressed. I eat the roti samosa from Vankol Krupa. Tonight I'll knock on her door.

Enrapture. Rend. Repeat.

"You've got some nerve."

I try to respond but words won't come. My mouth gapes like a koi, opening and closing with false starts.

Taja's lips are parted, her tongue pressed against the back of her clenched teeth. I have never known a variant of her to do this. As she did.

I should be leaning in, seizing this day and channeling her anger into my cause instead of standing here like a carp without the diem. I thought I was ready. Had stood and stared for an hour at the photos of us stuck to my fridge. We'd known each other for a year but a lot of that has been spent apart because she's—

"I turned down National Geographic for you. *National. Geographic.*"

—a photographer. Like my Taja before we learned of the Great Compression and enlisted.

"Hey!" Her eyes flash fury and she jabs an accusatory finger into my sternum. "Are you listening to me, Remington?"

"Not really." My voice cracks under the Herculean effort to do my damn job.

Taja recoils. She's the speechless one now. She steadies herself against the fact of her own doorframe. I wish she'd just slam the door in my face and end this.

We stand like that in silence for three or four days or maybe for six and a half seconds and I know I should just walk away, cross the hall, open then slam my own apartment door. But tears are welling in her green eyes shot with bronze and I can't look away.

"You..." She finds her voice but it shakes.

My novel memories inform the moment. So mundane. So everyday. We'd planned a long weekend together but instead I'd hidden in my apartment and ugly-cried for a three days. Recycle. Reuse. Reset.

"If you didn't want me," she finally hisses but it's venom-less, fang-less, submerged in loosed tears. "You could've just said so."

I should say, *You're right. I don't want you.* I should say, *People change. I've changed. We're over.* But I'm thrown, unsure. I've ended hundreds of us but not like this and never an us that seemed so much an us.

Instead I say, "Taja."

And something goes wrong. A storm cloud of emotion envelopes her expression and she draws herself up. Her pulse is leaping in her neck. My heart is pounding in my chest.

She closes her door in my face.

187

I stand staring at the unit number, wondering what I'd just seen, wondering how I should feel. Was I over-thinking this? Was I under-thinking it?

I run a quick checksum and yes, her name here is Taja. Not common for me to find but common enough.

I look down at the concrete floor. Perhaps my job here is done? Perhaps, for once, this love affair has already happened. I'm just here to see the end for once.

It's later that night and I'm still there. Not in the hallway but on the same world. I'm sitting on my low futon-style couch with dinner untouched and cold on the coffee table before me. I found black Levi's in my closet and a red V-neck tee. My feet are bare and my toe nails are pedicured and painted black.

From the moment I knocked on her door and she answered I've been off my game. The three day adjustment? Standard for me. But this dumb-founded inability to think clearly?

This Taja is just too close to my own.

Aren't they all my own? Or are none of them?

But I know this woman. I know her blue-black raven hair. Her full lips and thick brows. Her green-bronze eyes, full breasts and hips. Her job. Her voice. Her ferocity.

What else is the same?

I replay each word exchanged and analyze her intonation and body language. I try to stay detached and clinical. It certainly felt like we were—they were before me—deeply in love. Is that enough? Do I move on?

I shake my head hard. Get in the game, soldier! Buck up! Was I wearing thin? Was I becoming a shade of who I once was? Was I even that person anymore? My original body was long-since dead—as dead as this one will be when next I jump. (The normal reason for heartbreak.) Was it even possible to wear thin under these constantly renewing circumstances?

I knew that wasn't it. It wasn't so complicated and psychological. It was simple: She was too familiar.

If you didn't want me, you could've just said so.

I jerk ramrod straight. My not-my memories whisper to me. I cover my face with both my hands.

My job here is not done.

I can tell she's been crying but she answers the door anyway.

"May I come in?" I hold up a bottle of brandy bought in London and saved for the weekend I ruined.

Taja steps aside and pushes ribbons of hair back from her face. She says nothing. She looks paler than her olive complexion normally allows. Like she's had a freight.

I walk to her couch—brown and gold with soft cushions—and lift snifters from the sliding drawer under the center table. I tell myself I'm not disconcerted that I've done this before, a hundred lifetimes ago with a woman alarmingly the same.

Taja comes to stand at the entrance to the room, her arms crossed, her eyes wide as she watches me like one would watch a bird that had flown in the window.

I pour two fingers into two glasses and offer her one. My hand is steady. "Taja." I'm watching her intently. "I want you."

It isn't a come on. It isn't a sexual thing. It's an apology.

She should shake off her sense of abandonment and dread. She should reach toward me with long, strong hands that I know all too well. But she just watches me—the wild thing in her living room.

I set her snifter down on the table and sit down on the couch with my own.

"I got scared, love," I try the endearment on; not surprisingly, it sounds natural. "I'm not the brave one here."

I look at her. There is no pretense written on my face. I have an objective, yes, I have a mission but I also have a heart in my throat and a blush to my cheeks that's only partially from the two glasses of brandy I drank before coming over.

Taja's left eye twitches a little and she slowly cocks her head to the side. Who's the bird now?

"Say it again."

I stop mid-sip and look back up at her still standing in the archway. I hazard a guess, "I want you." But she's already shaking her head.

"Say my name."

I'm nervous, growing paranoid. I check not-my memories again. I inhale. I exhale. "Taja."

Her eyes close. She is so still I'm afraid something has gone terribly wrong. Some glitch in the matrix of space/time. Some hiccup or—

She sits down beside me, picks up her snifter and drinks.

I watch her look into her glass (it's good brandy) and then at me. She is unreadable but also more beautiful than I have ever seen her.

"I forgive you."

It feels like she's saying so much more.

The moon has risen and set and Taja's blouse is open, her long hair free, her head on my chest as we sit entwined with our empty bottle of brandy, the last two figs, and a single nankhatai on a cobalt plate.

"You're a good listener," she says, tracing the deep collar of my tee with her fingertips. Her words blend together just a little bit and I know she's drunk.

"Sometimes."

She makes a wordless sound of forgiveness. Love makes us forget as often as it makes us remember.

"I should probably get home," I murmur gently, able to lean in so easily now, to sink into this embrace of me wrapped around her.

I can't help my own small sound of pleasure as her fingers trail up my neck, along my jaw, and come to rest—butterfly-light—on my lips.

"I don't want you to leave." She whispers it so softly, so sadly.

I kiss her fingertips and draw her tighter. "Taja."

Her eyes sink shut. I feel her shudder. I reach for the cotton-soft embroidered wrap across the back of the couch but she turns in my arms and kneels between my thighs, facing me in our embrace.

"Remi." Her eyes search my face like she's memorizing me or searching for something she's not sure of. "I don't want you to leave."

I shudder this time. The room feels cold. Her eyes do not. The double meaning she can't possibly know is like something arctic or paranormal. Like a specter, lifeless and merciless.

I force a smile and touch her face. "It was the lark, the herald of the morn, no nightingale, my love."

Taja smiles back at me and her smile is genuine and so sweet my heart aches. How many decades have I missed that smile, seeing so many variations but never one quite as *right* as this. "You and your literary illusions."

"Those are the best ones."

"You're such a charmer."

"Prince Charming will come back and make you breakfast in the morning."

"I'd rather you be my princess."

Don't I know it. In all my jumps, I've only been a man twice and both times so was she.

We kiss goodnight and she tastes like brandy, figs, and shortbread with violet petals.

I close my door but don't lock it. My head is spinning and not from the brandy. Okay, maybe a little from the brandy. I don't want us to sleep together. I mean... *I do.* More than anything else in this moment I do but it feels... *wrong. Really* wrong.

This time.

I open my eyes when I realize I've closed them. Desperately my gaze darts. I busy my mind in the academia I find around me; I'm not surprised by the eight over-populated bookshelves crammed into my studio apartment. The colors printed on the spines form a collage of memories—half of which are mine across dozens of worlds—and lure me into a place of calm.

You and your literary illusions.

Once, when Taja's name was Kiki and her hair was lilac and teal, she said the same thing to me but followed it up by saying, *Half the time, I can't even find the book!* Because reflections don't always get the details right.

I've always loved to read. I don't actually remember learning how. It's just something I've always done. I feel solace with a book in my hands. Before I enlisted, I watched as Bradbury's *Fahrenheit 451* and *1984*'s Orwellian nightmare proved true. I watched humanity bend away from altruism and unity into demagoguery. The centre cannot hold.

I close my eyes again. I recite Yeats in my head and remember that in his early 1919 drafts, *The Second Coming* was called *The Second Birth*; if written today, it might have been *The Second Jump* or *The Thirtieth Leap.*

The age old question: Which is more valuable? Words or numbers.

While Shelley's 1826 *The Last Man* or Orwell's 1945 *Animal Farm* were alarmingly prescient in their insight into government fallibility during a worldwide pandemic and the willingness of the people to grant assumptive obedience in the service of tyranny, the numerous volumes of fact, fiction and foretelling penned by futurists did not, humorously enough, stand the test of their most invaluable commodity: Time.

In 1993, a futurist predicted we'd create super computers that so far surpassed us that human function would be irrelevant. In 2005, another futurist proposed that machine cognition would render common institutions needless.

In turns Pollyanna or Doomsayer, these town criers were forecasting the rise of Artificial Intelligence—a neuroscience/technology hybrid concept—that since its inception in the 1920s and subsequent popularization in the 1950s—has persevered as the Holy Grail and/or Boogeyman of moneyed men with too much time on their hands. Which is interesting since one prominent proponent of the destructive AI theory once said, *Time is meaningless when there's too much of it. Time is only valuable in limited supply.*

But the futurists were wrong. About everything.

I walk to my couch, almost forgetting to watch where I'm going. Maybe it's not exhaustion that closes my eyes; I dread bearing witness. I sink down and lie back.

AI didn't turn out to be our executioner but rather our liberation from universal extinction. It was a reservoir of algorithms that showed the watchmen approach was flawed, that solved global problems on a universal scale, that predicted the coming of the Great Compression. AI gave us data. And a data-driven society can make colossal change.

Instead of abandoning the Monster (because remember, Victor Frankenstein left his creation nameless) humanity rose to the maternal occasion and embraced what terrified us the most: We would accept the inevitability of dimensional collapse in a way we never fully accepted the climate crisis or the infertility epidemic. The odds were against us but Battalion after Battalion would deploy to align our reflective dimensions. If we could coordinate 4.669% of our closest parallels, they would consolidate into one and come out the other side intact.

When first I jumped, we were at T minus four hundred fourteen years until the Great Compression. Where are we now? Does it really matter? I'll jump and keep jumping until there's no reflection to jump into.

I just have to do my job.

It's just... my job seems especially hard today.

Exposition wears me out. That's why I love waxing academic; it's the best sleep aid I've found.

I fall asleep on the couch and dream of Arnold Palmer. Not the golfer (though once he said, *The most rewarding things in life are those that look like they can't be done.* which is quite apropos) but the Cambodian-American private that I trained with at Parris Island.

Palmer was a friend. As much of a friend as one could make when you know you only have days until your body unravels. We shared a desire for continence even while we shared the connection of kamikaze soldiers.

Palmer was scheduled to leave the day before me. He was the first person I knew more than casually who was scheduled to jump and I wanted to say goodbye. I snuck away to the Maw (the nickname we'd given the quantum well) and Palmer was outside the building, leaning back against the whitewashed concrete wall and looking... amused.

"Care to share the funny?" I leaned back beside him. We both stared straight ahead. No sound escaped the building at our backs.

"Got my mission," Palmer offered, still with a crooked grin. "I'm..." We'd all been told we weren't allowed to share our missions. Not with friends, family, lovers. But Palmer continued in his amused denial, "I'm killing a butterfly."

"No." My tone was ridiculously incredulous on several different levels. Palmer had never broken any rule of command; he wasn't one to be amused by anything. And killing a butterfly couldn't possibly save the human race.

"Yes."

Then we were both laughing. Laughing so hard I thought I'd pee my fatigues. It had to be a code or a hypnosis of some kind. It couldn't possibly be... that a trucker would emerge from a rest stop restroom and spot a Monarch, dead, on the sidewalk. Always having been a superstitious man, he would call dispatch and make up an excuse to abandon his rig, quit his job, and return home in time to stop a hate crime across the street. And the little boy he saved would grow up to be the man who wrote the final line of code that awoke our first AI and unfurled infinite algorithms.

Big or small. Sadistically insignificant or monstrously masochistic. Our missions were doled out in binary, translated by a second machine, then given to us without human intervention or opportunity for explanation, compliment or complaint.

Palmer turned to me. "Maybe they'll ask you to kill Krishna."

I think we laughed again but this time I just woke up.

Taja was standing in my open doorway holding a new bottle of Chhaang rum and a bag of masala dosa take out. She was soaked from sheets of rain, her wet locks like streaks of midnight sky plastered to her like a painter's strokes. She smiles at me, sweet and adoring. "You missed breakfast but how about dinner?"

I don't remember crossing the room but I do remember kissing her.

I wish the binary had told me to kill a god.

"I want you," I tell her. And this time, she knows exactly what I mean.

She is a molten creature beneath me. A living flame herself nonetheless caught in the light of two dozen (and one) fiery tongues. The candles around the room are red, orange, and buttercream. Her voice, her dance, her rise and fall are arresting, captivating, and so precisely, perfectly the Taja I know that more than once I forget when/where/who/what and with whom I am. If quicksilver were olive-gold, she would be an alchemist, transmogrifying my deep state strategy into carnal desire so sharp that I find myself willingly flayed.

She lays me bare and the only things between us are secrets.

I kiss her nape, her jawline. I weigh her hair, dry of rain but damp now with sweat and the tears that fall when you're turned inside out by passion. Unprompted, surprising myself, I ask, "Would you rather be romanced or ravished?"

She laughs at the unexpected and tugs me down beside her. "You want to talk?"

I play with her hair. "I want to know you better."

"You know me very well." She lifts one eyebrow, amused by me.

I wet my lips. Taste her. Fall in love. I tread carefully. "Never enough," I whisper over her ear and it's true. I am insatiable when it comes to her. All of her. Every aspect cast wide over countless dimensions.

"Ravished," she confesses, watching my expression. I think her favorite part of talking is watching my reactions; I've been told I have no poker face.

She continues, her eyes on my parted lips, my dilated pupils, the fast rise and fall of my chest. "Romance is so archetypal. Not contrived but filled with troupes like flowers and chocolate and candles." We both laugh a little as she motions to the candles she lit around her bedroom. "When you take me...." Her voices trails away and now she looks only at my mouth, her gaze cast down not in modesty but memory. "You make me feel wanted, desired, sought after. And somehow both sexy *and* strong!"

She laughs harder and I touch her face. "You *are* both."

"You're so controlled, so restrained normally," she adds carefully. "My lit professor love."

We kiss slowly, savoring each other. I think I taste like rum but Taja tastes like homecoming.

"You say my name differently."

I hold my breath but she says no more. We're so close, face to face, and she's watching me again more intently than I think anyone has ever watched me.

"Just... a little," she adds.

I manage to swallow. I manage to breathe. I don't manage to speak.

"I answered your question." She traces my collar bone, making it real to me. Shadows pool beneath her fingertips and in those small places I imagine secrets lie submerged like Dwarka under the sea. "Will you answer one from me?"

You just asked a question, I almost tease her in my nervousness, my apprehension. Instead I grow a spine and answer, "It's only fair."

I expect her to mull her options, to consider and contemplate. Instead, she asks immediately, "Should I feel safe with you?"

Ice water in my veins. The manifestation of dread. The tangible beast of fear.

I want to cry, *No! Run! Get up and leave me instead of loving me.*

But I say nothing. And that's how I knew I was still in it. I was shaken, bent low, but not broken.

"I will love you until the end of time." My not-answer satisfies her.

A month later, I'm still there—not in her bed but in her world—and she tells me she wants us to have a baby. Together.

I really need to leave.

I really can't.

We spend the weekend driving for hours both ways to spend thirty minutes in a new bookstore that dares to have a tiny section of queer books in the back corner of the shop. I love the way books are laid down on the shelves in India. No tilting sideways to read titles. No bowed or bent books even in humid environs.

We get chai on a busy street and walk together without touching. It was illegal to be gay in India until 2020.

"Your turn to start," I tell her. Our *Getting to Know You* game has continued these six months. It still amuses her and still surprises me.

"What does my name mean?"

"Crown," I answer without thinking.

Taja stops walking. Hers is a ghost smile, thin, obscured by something unspoken and invisible. "A brief moment in time."

I walk two steps before I realize she's stopped so now we face each other with four feet of empty space between us. We have moments like this one occasionally. Moments when she seems to be waiting for me to... what?

"What does Remington mean?" I counter with a jaunty smirk, deflecting, playing it off.

"Nothing," Taja tells me. "Just pretty sounds together."

She starts walking again and then we walk together. This world is more divergent and less divergent in the strangest ways.

What does that mean for me?

For us?

It's been a year. The monsoons have come again. We're wrapped in each other, angles and curves fitting like a single creature supine. Taja is luxury, royalty, reward. I am forgetting myself. Forgetting everything else. Everything but her.

I let go of my flat eight months ago and stacks of my books have grown like tree trunks of papyrus in every room of Taja's apartment. I listen to the rain, a constant roar like the ocean. I imagine a rain forest made of books. I imagine sheaves of paper instead of leaves, bookmarks instead of birds.

"Have you read about bifurcation theory?"

I shake my head but of course I have. Gods be damned. Just when I think I can forget….

Taja smiles and settles closer to me. This is the kind of thing she loves to do. To share some piece of newly discovered intellectual property. "It's a fundamental constant," she explains perfectly. "Anything with parabolic growth."

"Like life itself," I murmur.

"You *have* heard of it."

"Tell me more."

Taja shifts up on one elbow. Even naked and revealed, she is poised, composed and elegant. It's not easy to be elegant when unbuttoned. "You tell me."

I drown in her eyes. I don't want to speak. I want to lay beside her and fantasize about forests of books; I don't want to lie. So I don't.

"Periodic doubling," I explain, "occurs naturally. Until totals reach a saturation percentage and the doubling branches into two distinct patterns."

"Everything is patterns. Repeating," she adds, her gaze even more intent than a moment before.

What's happening?

"Then four branches, then eight. The branches grow at a set rate until—"

"Chaos."

I'm looking directly at her and yet she feels fathomless, endless, branching herself even as I watch her, becoming more complex with every moment. "Yes. Eventually, growth descends to chaos. But then it comes back. It simplifies and begins anew."

"It compresses."

"Where did you read this?" I blurt the words.

She doesn't look away from me. "I don't remember."

She's lying to me and I think it's the first time.

"Should I make us dinner?" I'm a master of deflection, breaking eye contact and turning away before she can—

"Stay."

I stay.

Taja is struggling. I see it now. She isn't fishing. She isn't searching. There's something she needs to say, not something she needs to hear. Her eyes study the sheets as if looking for just the right words.

"Remington..." Taja takes one of my hands in both of hers. She sits up straighter. Our touch imparts strength but still she hesitates. For long moments, we are still, together, while the world rages outside this room and inside my head.

"Remington," she starts again, then looks up at me. "I want this."

How powerful to hear that from someone. That proclamation

of authentic desire. I wonder why she seems so unsettled.

"I want this more than anything I've ever wanted in all my life and it's about time I do something for me!" A rush of words and emotion.

My heart sings. I shift to reach for her, to pull her back down beside me but she continues.

"But..."

Why is there a but?

"...I have to ask..."

Does she?

"...just so I know for sure..."

Know what?

"What will it be like without you?"

There it is.

Taja ignores the tears that fall down her face. Her body language, her tone of voice, nothing betrays her heart like those tears.

"Taja."

Her eyes close and a tide of additional tears are forced down her cheeks. "Remi. Don't speak."

I don't. She continues in another rush as if she's afraid she'll lose her nerve: "When the time comes, what will it feel like? Like being eaten up or drowned or pressed back into clay?"

I can't answer her but still she asks: "When all is done and there's only one world left, will I get to live my life with you? A you who isn't you... a me that isn't me."

"You know."

"I do."

And so we stare at one another in a way I have never looked at another human being for a century or more. "What gave me away?"

She can't or won't stop the grin that tugs up the corner of her mouth. "Two dozen languages are spoken in India with more than seven hundred dialects."

"The way I say your name."

Small wrinkles around her eyes. When did those appear? How long have I loved her? All my life it seems.

I sit up as I ask, "How long have you known?"

"As long as I've lived. My parents told me the story."

"The story?"

She takes my hand in a way I know so well. "The story of Taja Tangali. My namesake. Their gurumayi."

The bed, the floor, the building, the earth beneath the foundation gives way beneath me and only me and I feel myself falling. So unexpected. So new.

"She came to them during the monsoons when first my parents were married. It was late at night but my father was a very spiritual man and he let her in. He knew she was something... *other*."

"What—" I choke on my shock. "What... did she look like?"

"A lot like me."

"But you're not...?"

"No, Remington." Her smile is sad; I regret implying. "I'm not the Taja from your timeline."

I can't help it. I don't want to hurt the woman before me but my eyes sink shut and I ignore but can still feel my tears. For just a moment... for just a moment.

"You want me to be."

Not a question so I don't answer.

I feel her shift beside me on the bed. "She could be somewhere still. Out there in the world."

"No." I open my eyes already shaking my head. "There can be only one." Only one jumper in a dimension at a time. Only one variant of a person at a time.

Taja nods. Understanding enough. "I'm sorry."

I am without words. I just look at her.

She asks without accusation, "You're used to this? What you do."

"I've had a lot of time to adjust."

My fingers have closed around the sheet, grabbing fistfuls, white-knuckled, perhaps trying to anchor myself, perhaps trying to cling to the past... to an hour ago... to ten minutes ago before this conversation.

Taja places one hand over one of mine. "Time heals all wounds but not if you keep cutting the same place."

I flail. I'm not good with spontaneity, with unplanned and brutal blindsiding. (I'm also a hypocrite.) I blurt, "Why would she do this?"

"You tell me."

But I can't. My mind is completely blank. My senses under water or beneath a heavy layer of fog. I look down at her hand on mine. I wait.

Taja says more, "She told my parents someone would come. During the monsoons. After they were gone. And we would fall in love."

I sneak a look at her. Her expression isn't hurt or sorrowful but resigned, melancholy.

"And because of us, because of small things—the streets we walked or things we bought, children we'd raise or books you'd write, photographs I'd take—humanity would survive chaos."

No pressure. The thought blooms with disparaging sarcasm. *No self-importance.*

Aloud I say, "The Great Compression."

Taja nods once. Adds, "Somehow those small things would

help this world *align and...*"

Silence. We meet eyes. "What else?"

"She said you'd leave me."

"I'll never leave you." Said automatically, autonomously. And also not true. Only partially true. Not true at all in any way. "I always return to you." Amended.

"But it's not me."

And there it is.

She sees me. I see her.

"Not her either."

She's right. I don't want her to be but she is.

Again with the confusion, the shock, the blurting, "Why would she tell you?"

"Because she wanted me to choose, Remington."

"But we did! We—"

"But *I* didn't."

Right. Of course.

She bows her forehead to mine and whispers, "Perchance to love."

Her own literary illusion and a dark one at that. Perchance the dreamless sleep after death? Perchance the sleepless nights after love is lost.

"A chance you're willing to take?" I ask her.

Taja leans back a little, sizing me up. "Now you ask consent? After how many worlds?"

Touché. That expression, that sass. So familiar. "Are you sure you're not—"

"Yours?" She smiles at me. "I am. Her? I'm not. And you're not my Remi."

My mouth opens. No words. Then only, "I'm sorry."

"I wasn't in love with my Remington."

Haven't I had enough surprises for one day? A hundred lifetimes?! "But—"

"She was my best friend. And she was also very straight."

I erupt with laughter and Taja joins me. We both know it's awkward and sad but that part remains unspoken and we laugh because it's a release we can manage.

We wind up shifting closer together, moving into one another's arms—for the last time?—and leaning back against the emerald green pillows I bought her at the bazaar.

I try for honesty, I reach for transparency for the first time in too many years. "Each mission objective is different. The same end goal but different means of getting there. I... I just have to love you."

Taja leans her head down a little lower; she's a head taller than me, after all. The green of her eyes is amplified by the silk pillows. "And leave me. Over and over again."

Collateral damage. But I don't say it.

"Is my heartbreak what keeps us all alive?"

Her honesty puts mine to shame. "I don't know."

Taja nods. She doesn't move away from me.

"Perhaps," she's thoughtful, pondering. "*Her* mission was to tell me. To let *me* choose." Taja looks at me pointedly. "To let you choose. Again."

I hear my own gasp. *Pick again, Remington.* "Oh."

"Remington." She kisses me. "Don't leave."

It may be that love will be our downfall. It may be that Taja—my Taja—has gone rogue across the timelines. That she exists in the fringe of chaos. That she's rewriting the rules. I have no way of knowing.

All that I know is this: I can cease to breathe but I cannot cease to love her. No longer can I walk—or fly or fall or jump—away from her side. To hell with everyone else.

“I want you.”

Let stardust run through the hourglass. Let humanity go to seed. And let those seeds plant a hundred million new worlds.

Time can be unraveled but not Taja Tangali.

Never my love.

An Interview with Jennifer DiMarco

When did you start writing and why?

I started writing seriously (six to ten hours a day) when I was ten years old and my first therapist suggested I try journaling to help me communicate better. My parents—I have two moms—bought me a 300-page blank book and I decided to write a 50,000-word novel where women were oppressed for generations but finally rose up in both peaceful and not so peaceful ways.

(If you're wondering how a ten year old had that much time to write every day and still attend school, I will admit that it was this same time that I started sleeping less and less and it was only about a year before I was bussing an hour to and an hour from school.)

Why this all began was touched on in *Terms of Service*, my story for Emerge November which appears in the Emerge Autumn edition. What I didn't touch on was: I was an incredibly late reader and never learned phonics.

The elementary school I attended believed in the

memorization approach to reading. Hanging from giant jump rings, students carried "keywords"—index cards hole-punched in one corner. A teacher would write a word we liked on each card. At any time, any teacher (the entire school—first through sixth grade—was open concept without walled classrooms) could ask us to start reading (reciting) our keywords and if we "read" one of the words wrong, the card was ripped in half and thrown away. Looking back, I'm not surprised I couldn't read a sentence—let alone read (or write!) an entire book until I was in fifth grade.

I wrote that first novel in a personal shorthand—building sentences and characters with misspelled words as much as with symbols and personal cues that would remind me what word I wanted there. My vocabulary was thick with words parroted from adults and I was constantly being praised for my eloquence and comprehension... but my ability to both encode and decode were severely lacking. And while I continued my educational experience at small, alternative, arts-focused schools, it wasn't until taking Latin in high school that words started to really make sense.

It probably comes as no surprise that I was adamant that both my children learn phonics—even though they both hated it! I'm very pleased that both of them spell better than I do.

Which authors or books influenced you the most as a writer?

Before I answer this question, I would be remiss not to mention: I love science fiction because I love science. Science has always turned on my creative brain; it excites and incites me. Physics, chemistry and mathematics concepts have been the flashpoint of all of my best work.

And now for an answer: While I enjoy a good action adventure or mystery novel as much as the next reader, I do see these as escapism and I don't read to escape. (For escapism I tend to turn to painting, boxing, hiking, or woodworking.)

Because my greatest literary love is surrealist science fiction (what has come to be called "New Weird" in the industry) my rare and precious pleasure reading is also the reading that inspires and incites me. Namely:

Richard Calder (*The Dead Things Trilogy*)
Jeff VanderMeer (*The Southern Reach Trilogy*)
Charles Stross (*Singularity Sky, Glasshouse, Accelerando*)
Clifford A. Pickover (*Time: A Traveler's Guide*)

Before someone calls out the fact that there are no women on this list, yes, I am very aware of that. I wish there were more women writing in the field of surrealist science fiction. And while I adore the arching ideas and characters in work by Octavia E. Butler and Nnedi Okorafor (specifically The Xenogenesis Trilogy and The Binti Trilogy, respectively), Butler and Okorafor feel familiar and welcome to me, and when I read, I want to be unseated, to question what I know and expand my perception.

I will say that I recently read Amal el-Mohtar and Max Gladstone's novella, *This Is How You Lose the Time War*, and will absolutely be exploring more work by both of them so perhaps Amal will be the woman writer I've been looking for. (Though I'm very glad the phrase "woman writer" is no longer bandied about the way it was when I was younger and was afraid to write under my name, opting for the genderless "J. DiMarco" for the first ten years of my career.)

I will admit, I'm not someone who reads or enjoys everything written by an author; I can't stand campy, B-grade humor or high fantasy or formula mysteries or romance—the list goes on. There are way more genres I don't care for than I do! I am far more inspired by specific books and stories than by authors themselves and their entire body of work. But this may be because I tend to enjoy eclectic authors who create in diverse genres.

I think the only other authors I would add to my list of influences would be the poet Adrienne Rich (*Fact of a Doorframe*) and the novelist Jeanette Winterson (*Written on the Body*). I suppose there are two women for my list of authors who made me see the world in a new way.

Which authors or books had the biggest impact on you as a person?

In contrast to the work that influenced me as a writer, the authors and prose that were influential to me personally are a bit more wide-ranging in several ways. With sociopolitical commentary, explorations of power and recovery, and authentic journeys of grief and isolation, these are novels, nonfiction, and short stories by a spectrum of authors.

Neal Stephenson (*Snow Crash, Diamond Age*)
Leslie Feinberg (*Stone Butch Blues*)
Pat Califia (*Doc and Fluff*)
Minnie Bruce Pratt (*S/He*)
Katherine V. Forrest (*Emergence of Green*)
Camille Paglia (*Sexual Persona*)
Lauren Wright Douglas (*In the Blood*)
Herb Montgomery (*The Apple and the Envelope*)
Taro Yashima (*Crow Boy*)
Katsuhiro Otomo (*Akira*)
Philip K. Dick (*Do Androids Dream of Electric Sheep*)
James Patrick Kelly (*Think Like a Dinosaur*)

I think, more than anything else, the inherent dichotomy of my life is on display in that list. What a wonderful sense of freedom!

For more than thirty years, I've run a 501(c)3 nonprofit dedicated to bringing the work of marginalized authors, musicians, filmmakers, and game designers to the public. All work that speaks to the human condition honestly and that strives to break stereotypes and clarify misconceptions is eligible—whether created by a conservative Christian or a liberal social justice activist. And while I don't think any of my artisans wish me ill, I am very aware that many of them would not hesitant to vote for a candidate who would consider it a great victory to annul my marriage to my wife.

To say that I have dedicated my life to empowering and amplifying the voices of storytellers who are dynamically different from me—all while presenting only the G-rated "Earth Mother" side of myself to them—would be an oversimplification but also true.

Which of your original twelve Emerge stories are you most pleased with?

When the Emerge project began, we were told the goal was to turn in our best prose every month. I took this very seriously. On average, for work, I write 45,000 words a month. (Which was a fun average to find over ten months in 2020.) The grant applications, emails, letters, reports, and scripts that make up that word count often leave me wanting to do anything except write more. I willingly dive into every CFO task on my desk—from taxes to budget sheets— just for a chance to play with numbers for a change. Yet every month in 2019, the first project I completed was my story for Emerge.

My goal was always the same: That each story be better than my last... or at least be the best thing I wrote that month. So while I consider "When Time Unravels" or "When Wanda Woke the World" my best stories, it was "Social Box" that was made into a feature film in 2020 and it was "Unilateral Agreement" that I'm most asked to present as a guest author.

If I absolutely had to pick a personal favorite, it would have to be "Lost in Translation."

Which of your original twelve Emerge stories did you find the most difficult to write?

This question is a little easier to answer. When writing "Fireworks" I stalled about five hundred words in. I knew exactly the story I wanted to tell but my own life experiences kept wanting to infiltrate and obliterate the character's. It took me longer than I care to admit to excise my demons so I could write about Geraldine's.

The strange thing is that while the hardest to write, "Fireworks" is not my least favorite story nor do I consider it, ultimately, unsuccessful. That backhanded award goes to "Statement Island." I consider "Statement Island" to be a failure because the medium is indisputably wrong.

The story is set adjacent to a fictional locale my wife and I considered exploring together in a team-written, episodic novel. The characters might reappear but the focus would be on the lawless wonderland Faregrounds. I was so enthralled with my original concept of Faregrounds that I couldn't get it out of my head. But I also knew the full arch I wanted to explore wouldn't fit in a short story and I'd promised to develop it with Brianne—not craft it alone for a solo project like Emerge. The resulting compromise with my own brain was "Statement Island" and perfectly illustrates why I'm not a big fan of compromise.

What book on writing do you recommend?

This is such an intensely personal choice. Instantly I want to say Natalie Goldberg's *Writing Down the Bones* and William Strunk Jr.'s *The Elements of Style*. But I think far more important than which book or books you read is that you actually take the time to educate yourself about your craft.

This is perhaps my biggest pet peeve in this field. So many people think being a writer is just writing. (Others think that just having a "one of a kind idea" is being a writer.) And maybe writing is indeed all it takes. But the way I was raised and educated in this particular art, anyone can be a writer... but being a writer is very different from being an author.

Arrogant? Stuck up? I hope not because it doesn't take a degree or special tools or an expert editor in your back pocket to become an author. It does take discipline, research, more research, and growth. But I'll get to that in the next question.

What advice would you give an unpublished writer?

It amazes me to this day how many people (how many published writers!) don't perform their due diligence. If a lawyer or doctor slacked off the way I see so many authors do on a daily basis there would be hell to pay or even lives lost. These authors are very lucky that their only consequences are tiny royalty checks.

I suppose, ultimately, these are writers, not authors. They are willing to write—maybe even write up a storm!—but they are not willing to handle the myriad of other tasks that make a writer into an author.

"Some people just want to write. They just want to be writers. Not everyone wants to be an author." My seventh grade creative writing teacher first said that to me. And this is why I still count many writers among my friends. Because some receive all the joy and fulfillment they want just by putting pen to paper, just by crafting with words. I value and appreciate their passion for prose.

But I'm going to pretend that this question is asking: "I want to transform from a writer to an author. How do I do that?" This is my advice—just my opinion—on exactly that.

1. Take a creative writing class... without telling anyone you're published already (if you are). Don't go into the class thinking you know everything and don't share your laurels or you'll wind up on a pedestal and won't get real feedback. Pick a night class, community college class, or continuing education class with lots of peer critique and sharing. Go into the class determined to learn at least one invaluable thing.

2. Select and read at least two books on the craft—one written by an author that touches on the writing life and one written by an editor. Keep in mind that you need to know the rules of punctuation, formatting and grammar so that you know when it's okay to break or bend them.

3. Research! Research! Research! When writers say they don't read in their genre, I immediately consider them to be immature. Imagine a doctor saying, "I didn't do an internship. Or talk to other doctors. Or research the procedures I'll be specializing in. I just do my own thing." What I really hear when writers don't read is, "I don't like to read. I'm better than anyone else out there already. There is nothing more for me to learn."

Not only must you be educated in your genre but you must also be knowledgeable about the publishers and supporting magazines and blogs who publish in your genre. That's the second kind of research.

The third plea for research: God—and good fiction—is in the details. One of the most cringe-worthy things I've run into is when a writer will quote a statistic in a story that has been disproved or worse: Debunked. Hearsay is not fact. As a matter of fact (pun intended) if your boss at the cafe says, "Cherry pie is the most popular pie in America. Pitch the cherry." That may sound like a statement of fact but it's still just opinion. Until the fact has been verified by a third party or accepted as an industry standard across an industry, you're just spouting opinions (at best) or fake news (at worst).

Did you work as a zoo-keeper for thirty years? You can say, "In my experience as a zoo-keeper between 1973 and 2003, the penguins were the most popular animals." But you shouldn't make the statement, "The year was 2020 and penguins were the most popular exhibit."

Due diligence. Do your research and know the truth. Not just opinions, hearsay or rumors. Not just what you want to be true.

4. Write every day. It can be a journal entry, a personal letter or email, or on-going work on a story. (Technical writing, marketing copy, reports or writing for work doesn't count.) Do not allow yourself to have days when you don't write. Remember Malcolm Gladwell's statement about 10,000 hours of practice resulting in mastery? I think we all realize that's simply not true but it is a great start. Every minute helps.

5. Quality. Not quantity. I used to feel jealous when a peer was writing 6,000 words a day while also working an eight hour job. Then I saw their work.

Slow down. Edit and revise as you go. Don't be afraid to delete and start again. I call this my "active draft."

6. Struggle with spelling? Grammar? Punctuation? Or maybe you just want to catch more mistakes and create cleaner work? Consider a paid subscription to Grammarly (which catches more than the free version and can be applied to a word processing document).

7. Read your work aloud slowly and dramatically to yourself and revise more. I call this my "second draft."

8. When completed with a story or novel, take a week or more away from it completely and then come, read it over silently and revise it again. If you're finishing a story on the deadline, you're already a week late. I call this pass my "final draft."

9. Send your "final draft" to at least two people who love to read in your genre and who are willing to give you controlled critiques. What is a controlled critique? This is when you send your final draft and five to ten specific questions for someone. Examples:

- Do you find Susan likeable?
- Did you come across any plot holes or things you felt were unrealistic?
- Does Tony need a dog or cat to soften his image? A turtle?
- Was it believable that Kate didn't call the police right away?

Don't make your beta readers work too hard by giving them generic, nonspecific questions. Be smart enough and know your work well enough to spot where problems might lie and ask those questions. How will you know how to spot these problems? By being well-read in your genre.

I call these readers my "master readers" and I select them carefully so that I know and trust their insight. Make any changes suggested that you agree make the story stronger... even if it means you have to throw out a whole chapter or make another major change. Don't be afraid of hard work.

10. Last but not least, I never hire a freelance editor and I have never been asked to. My work has seen three drafts (plus any revisions made after your master readers make suggestions) before it ever goes to the editor at my publisher. Only the opinion of that editor matters to me. He or she will determine if the work is publishable.

Do you have a "dream project" as a writer? What would it be?

I think every fan reading this interview is shouting, "The release of *The Wind Trilogy*!" While all three volumes of the trilogy were actually written as one tome in 1989, the original publisher (and both subsequent publishers) divided the epic into three books and only the first two were ever released.

And while life (raising and educating two children, facing illness, having a time-consuming job) has delayed the final "Author Approved" edition of the work, I gently like to remind people that I wrote *Escape to the Wind, Fall Through the Sky,* and *Drinking Silver Wine* when I was sixteen. How would you feel about internationally publishing something you wrote when you were sixteen when you're forty-seven?

If you haven't grown and changed and matured and improved as an author, you might feel excited and delighted to release your teenage prose. But that isn't who I am or where I am in my career.

At first, I told my current publisher and editor that I would not feel comfortable releasing *The Wind Trilogy* until I had a current novel ready to publish simultaneously. In this way, people could see the journey I've taken over the last thirty-one years.

But in the end, *Body of Work*—the compilation of my thirteen stories written for Emerge—will be the work released alongside the trilogy. Another compromise. But one I'm more comfortable with.

My dream project would be a novel I began several years back that explores what it means to be sentient and why happiness and contentment are not synonymous. I wrote the first 10,000 words and then made the mistake of allowing the work to be read by another author who said, "The quality is astronomical. The tension and richness of the language is almost painful to read. You'll never be able to keep this up. Dial it back. Phone in a few scenes."

Never, ever, tell someone to dumb their work down. Why?

Because too many writers will listen to you and do it! The "dumbing down" of art—specifically prose—adds to the dumbing down of us as a people. The National Center for Educational Statistics reported in 2020 that 21% of adults in the United States (about 43 million) are illiterate or functionally illiterate. That statistic breaks my heart.

The original twelve Emerge stories were written in 2019. In 2020, we all experienced a global pandemic. Did the pandemic impact your writing? How?

I definitely had less time to write during 2020. My focus had to shift to paying the bills, aiding our at-risk artisans at work, and spending every remaining hour applying for grants, creating safe events and platforms, and organizing a rotation of the Board of Directors at Blue Legacy.

But all the same, I managed to sneak in some projects that were very special to me: In March, I wrote a children's book, *When Longneck Learned to Love*, about a small dinosaur learning self-love and my son, Maxwell, illustrated it. Then in August, my daughter, Faith, illustrated my children's poem, *Take Flight!*, about cute little fruit bats and it was published as a children's book. Finally, in October, *My Patchwork Heart*, a children's book about a woman who finds a dog who may or may not be real but who, nonetheless, teaches her that the things we love don't wear out, they just get worn in, was released—also with illustrations by Faith.

Of course, I also wrote *When Time Unravels*, my final story for Emerge. And I was hired to write two feature films in 2020 and seven short films.

Overall, I found writing hard in general in 2020 because my head was full of noise. This resulted in me needing to tuck myself away into absolute quiet when writing. I normally have a song that matches the ambiance of the piece I'm writing and I'll listen to that through headphones on repeat until I'm done writing but that wasn't possible in 2020. I hope that skill returns as the world heals and we all slowly start to move forward because my home is rarely quiet!